Sarah's Legacy

IT'S IN THE STARS

To Ruth

Enjoy

Mary Lynn

Mary Lynn

Edited by Danielle Patricio

Cover Designed by BYWR Graphics

Dedication

I dedicate this book to my family and the fans of my first book "The Forgotten Life of Sarah Grady." Also, to my granddaughter Danielle Patricio who is my amazing editor and my marvelous daughter Julie Moore who became my copy editor and formatted the book.

Note from the Author

With diligent research I have been able to track some of Sarah's activities after she was driven out of her home in disgrace in 1921. I had to imagine events but the general outline of her later life is true.

Sarah Grady was a product of her time believing that the stars could chart the direction of her life. At first a non-believer, she succumbed to the 1920's trend of society women leading their lives through astrology. Even our country's first ladies sought advice from their "Madams".

Today our population has the freedom to believe or not, but we have been left a legacy of celestial science that is hard to ignore.

PROLOGUE

Fairlawn Cemetery

Decatur, Illinois 2015

It was autumn. In Decatur's second oldest cemetery the hundred year old trees were flooded in bright colors. Carl who was the grave digger/grounds keeper was enjoying the beauty nature had bestowed on the peaceful grounds when he was interrupted by a friend.

"Hey, Al. Whatcha doin 'out here?" asked Carl.

"Well, you cemetery guys don't seem to know what goes on under the dirt, so I'm here to find out," said Al.

"You witchers think you know it all. I will say though, you've been proven right most of the time," replied Carl.

"What do you mean 'most of the time'? I'm right all the time," declared Al with a smile.

Carl, a grave digger, and Al, a grave witcher, stood behind a large granite tombstone in peaceful Fairlawn Cemetery. Al often brought his witching skills to the cemetery when the administration wanted to learn what was under the surface at various burial sites. He claimed to be able to tell whether or not a space was occupied, and if occupied, he could tell the gender of the body. He had been helpful for many years in revealing what no one could see underground.

"What did the boss ask you to do now back in this old section?" asked Carl.

"Not the boss. I'm here to meet a lady who has some questions about William Grady's site. I checked with the office and the Grady plot has places for three graves: William, his wife Esther, and a Sam Elwood. I guess she just wants verification," said Al.

A flashy but older car pulled to the side of the road by the Grady monument and a mature lady walked toward the duo.

"Here she comes", said Carl. "I'll leave you two to your magic."

The lady held out her hand, "Nice to meet you, Al."

"What would you like to know?" asked Al.

"I am on a mission to find William Grady's first wife Sarah and my quest has led me to this cemetery. I just want you to tell me if there is a body buried in every one of the three Grady spaces and whether the body in each place is a man or a woman," said the lady.

This sounded very easy to Al. He took his "witching wire" and started with the first grave on the left as one faced the monument. His wire fell to the right side. "There's a male buried here."

"Good," said the lady. "That's where William should be buried."

Taking a few steps further, Al's wire fell to the left. "There's a female buried here."

"Yes, that's Esther his second wife."

The lady tensed with anticipation as Al approached the third site which was to the side of the monument with no exterior marking. Al held up his witching tool which fell to the left. "There's another female buried here."

Visibly shaken the lady asked, "Are you sure that there is a female in the last site? Would you try that one again?"

Dutifully Al complied. Again he reiterated, "No doubt. It's a woman buried in this last site. I don't know what is going on because I checked with the office and they have a male, Sam Elwood, being interred in the last site. But my wire never lies. I don't know who it is, but it's a female."

"That's what I needed to know. Thank you for your help, Al," said the lady as she quickly retreated to her car and drove away.

Seeing that the lady had left, Carl came back to see what had happened. "Did ya 'find out what the lady wanted to know?"

"I guess. But Sam Elwood doesn't seem to be here like the office information says. There's a woman buried in his place. "

"Is that lady her relative?" asked Carl.

"I don't know for sure, but I don't think so. She seemed to think that Sam Elwood was here for sure. If he is… maybe he's below the woman? If that were the case my wire would not pick him up."

"Should we tell the office about the mix-up or whatever it is?"

Al thought for a minute and then said, "No. I don't think we should. The lady was really upset. Let her do what she will with the information I gave her. I hope she finds what she's looking for."

CHAPTER 1

Where is Sarah?

Decatur, Illinois May 18, 1921

William sat rigidly in his coach seat on the midnight train from Chicago to Decatur. Usually he reserved a sleeping car, but tonight there would be no sleep. He gazed out the window at the dark landscape as he clenched and unclenched his fists. He opened then slammed shut his briefcase. His business in Chicago was finished yesterday, but he had been unable to make himself go home.

Home! What would it be like without her? How could he face his business associates... his friends? Slowly untangling his six foot two frame from the small train seat, he walked down the aisle to get a drink of water. That didn't help. He marched back to his seat. Breathing deliberately, he attempted to relieve the knot in his stomach. That didn't work either. He recognized his internal problem as rage.

What time was it? Two A.M. The police would still be guarding the house so she couldn't get inside. He wondered where she would go. She could have left town with that trashy car salesman or spent the night at June's house. It didn't matter to him, he told himself. The knot in his stomach got tighter. *Get a grip, Grady.*

By the time the train pulled into the station at Decatur, it was six o'clock in the morning and he had managed a bit of control over his mental state.

Calling his ever faithful servant James on the lobby phone, he simply said, "Come get me."

William stood outside and prayed none of his acquaintances would be around the station this time of the morning. He recognized he looked every bit as bad as he felt and would not be able to make small talk with anyone. However, the station was deserted and before long James pulled up in the car.

For the first few blocks of the drive neither of them said a word. Then William broke the silence, "Are the police still at the house?"

James studied his employer, trying to assess his mood before he answered. "Yes, Mr. Grady. They said they would stay until you got home."

"Good."

They rode in silence the rest of the way to the Grady house.

As the car pulled into the driveway, William experienced a strange sensation. He felt weak. William J. Grady... weak? He was Secretary/Treasurer of Faries Manufacturing Company, President of the Chamber of Commerce, President of the Board of the Country Club of Decatur, President of the Decatur Club, and a director on the boards of Walrus Manufacturing Company and several other organizations... But right now, he did not feel whole... without the love of his life, his spirited balance, the only one who ever matched his stride in intellect and ambition. The beautiful, enigmatic Sarah.

 Usually the trip down the drive to his splendid home drained all the stress away from him. But now the police car that stood parked by the garage only heightened his internal upset.

"James, tell the police to leave. I don't need them anymore and I don't want to talk to them," snapped William.

James did as he was told. He harbored great concern for the man who had employed him for eleven years. Never had he seen him in this state. Yes, Mr. Grady had a temper, but this was different. This man was enraged, but defeated, broken.

The police went out the back door as William came in the front. He stepped into the entry hall and checked the grandfather clock that had stood there ever since the Grady's moved in. The hanging light reflected an Arts and Crafts mood which he had insisted upon when they built their dream home. This was his hallway, but somehow it seemed like a different place entirely.

"Did she attempt to get anything from the house last night?" asked William.

"No, everything was quiet. One of the neighbors called to ask if everything was alright and I just said yes," replied James.

"Tell our, uh MY, friends and business associates that I am unavailable to speak to anyone right now."

James considered his new assignment. *Running social interference is not what I signed up for. Mrs. Grady kept the house operating. But I can't leave Mr. Grady now. All the other servants have been fired; Miss Sarah's maid, the cook, and the gardener. He'll need help to overcome this recent chain of events and I'm the only one who can help him recover. There's no one else. He seems unhinged.* Outwardly, James just nodded his head in agreement.

William poured himself a drink and sat in his big upholstered chair in the library. He wanted to crush the tumbler in his palms, but refrained.

Instead, he studied the bookshelves as he questioned what had happened to his perfect life. Getting no answer from the inanimate objects, he tried to make sense of the events that had taken place over the last month. Pouring another drink, he reflected.

My gorgeous, sophisticated wife had a great mind for business. She helped me win over my clients and advance on a track to become the next president of Faries Manufacturing. She entertained for me and did anything else I asked of her. How could she do this to me? To us?

I thought her declarations of being through doing my bidding and entertaining were mere womanly hysterics for attention. Why did she act that way? Maybe I bullied her a little, but only when she wouldn't do what was needed. As my wife she should obey me. I gave her everything, jewelry, vacations at the finest resorts, clothes from Paris, standing in the community! She was an orphaned divorcee for God's sake! What else could she possibly want?

He poured more brandy into his glass.

William had realized the gravity of the situation when Sarah began to drink heavily. As a rule, she did not even drink socially. Despite his disapproval she had become part of the temperance movement and worked hard to, as she claimed, "keep alcohol from harming people's lives."

She became defiant. Every time I told her to do something, she refused to obey. Like the night she dressed for a business dinner at the country club. I felt her choice of an outfit reflected an inappropriate image. Yes, I shouldn't have ripped the dress she had chosen off of her, but I merely wanted her to wear the proper attire. She refused to put on what I selected and go to the dinner. Made me suspicious. Why didn't she care what I thought? I wondered if she still loved me or even respected our marriage vows. Was she having an affair? If she were to be unfaithful to me, I promised myself I would knock some sense into her.

From time to time in their marriage of eighteen years, he had wondered if she was being unfaithful to him. But she was such a dedicated wife and he loved her so much that he couldn't believe she would do anything wrong. Besides, her first husband had devastated her by an unfaithful act. William had been positive Sarah would not repeat those actions.

The clock in the library struck ten o 'clock and William jerked awake. He had dozed off for an hour or so due to a lack of sleep last night and the brandy he had consumed. For a moment he could not apprehend what was going on. It was morning. *Why was he in the library at this time of day? Where was Sarah?*

As he rose from his chair, the reality of the situation came flooding back to him. He shouted, "James, where are you?"

"Right here, Mr. Grady," responded James stepping into the library.

"Has Sarah been trying to get in the house?"

"No, sir. I haven't seen anything of her. Many people have called though wanting to speak to you. I just told them you were resting."

'Tell them I am unavailable! I'm not an invalid! Christ!'

William was back in the present and painfully aware of what was going on. "Where's the newspaper? Was there anything in it about our divorce trial yesterday?"

James hesitated, but knew he had to answer. "Well, yes, but I don't think you really want to read it. Maybe later…"

"Give me the newspaper."

James went into the kitchen and retrieved the paper. Wishing the account of Mrs. Grady's infidelity and her arrest had not been the headlines on the front page, James realized there was no saving Mr. Grady from the shame and scandal. Handing him the paper,

James tried to say something that could soften the situation. "The article doesn't tell about the court proceedings. Just about her arrest."

"That's what I told the police to do, just give the newspaper an accounting of her arrest. Well, at least people know why I filed for divorce."

James tried to busy himself in the room so he would not leave Mr. Grady alone while he read the paper. He took books off of the shelf and busily put them back again. Instead of shouting, William was quiet after absorbing what the paper considered the news of the day. Not knowing what he could say to ease the situation, James offered, "I don't know what happened to her, but I do recognize she was a lady who ran a great household and loved you very much."

William scowled. "I don't believe that anymore," said William as he hid his face in the newspaper. "People will only see that she has made a fool of me. I am ruined. Are you sure she hasn't tried to get into the house?"

CHARLES NEWLON AND MRS. W. J. GRADY PAY FINE AND DISAPPEAR

Charles T. Newlon, an automobile salesman, and Mrs. W. J. Grady, of Millikin place, were arrested in a room in 258 North Main street about 9:30 o'clock last evening. Arraigned before Justice Noble on disorderly conduct charges on both state and city warrants, they pleaded guilty, paid fines totaling $74.80 and were released.

Mr. Grady, who was in Chicago, was apprised of the arrest by a telephone message from the police. He requested that publicity be not spared and that nobody be allowed to enter his home before his return. Two police were stationed at the residence all night. He left Chicago last evening and was due to arrive this morning.

"Sarah Gray of Maroa."

The arrest was made by a squad of five policemen, headed by Captain Cline who gained entrance to Newlon's room at the southeast corner of Main and William streets. The couple were in scant attire when found.

They were taken at once to the police station and questioned. Mrs. Grady was suffused in tears, but finally was able to recover her self-possession. She gave the name of Sarah Gray of Maroa, age 44. Newlon gave his own name, and his age as 38.

Drive Away in Car.

After paying the fines the couple left, and disappeared toward the north in Mrs. Grady's car. It is understood that their movements had been under investigation for three months. The raid followed a tip that Newlon had been seen to enter Mrs. Grady's car and drive to his room last evening. Mrs. Grady is thought to have been in the room practically all the afternoon.

Mrs. Grady has been prominent in welfare work and society in Decatur. Mr. Grady is sales manager for the Faries Mfg. Co. Newlon is said to have been employed by the Charles Bradley Motor Co. He was formerly a waiter in a Decatur restaurant.

Reports of an improper relationship between the prominent society woman and the automobile salesman had been a subject of gossip for several weeks. Apparently they did not reach the ears of friends of Mrs. Grady, but they were common knowledge among associates of Newlon.

Sarah Grady Arrest Article - Decatur Review / May 18, 1921

CHAPTER 2

Sarah is Gone

Afternoon May 18, 1921

William got out of his chair, steadied himself, and raced up the stairs. James had trouble keeping up with him. The forsaken, defeated husband suddenly transformed into an aggressive combatant.

"James, open the windows in our bedroom. I'm going to throw out all of these ridiculous frivolities of Sarah's."

William's face was bright red like many men after they have had too much to drink. In this case, it seemed to James as if rage had the upper hand over the liquor and he was concerned about the very human master he saw before him.

James said, "Why don't you rest now and I'll spend the day gathering all Mrs. Grady's things. Maybe she'll send for them and …"

"If she sends for them, you will tell her that I have destroyed everything she owned."

"Please, let me dispose of them properly. What would the neighbors think if they saw all her things littering the lawn?"

"Open the windows!"

James complied and William began to throw everything that had belonged to his wife out of the bedroom window. Out went the expensive dresses. He took delight in tossing out the red one she wore on two occasions to his business dinners. He had believed the dress was too revealing for her to wear for his clients, but now the thought of how beautiful she looked in it crept into his mind.

Out went the fancy robes. Why did his memory keep interfering with the process of removing her from his world? All he could think of as one of the robes flew to the ground was how he had chastised her for spending almost thirty-five dollars on that garment. It wasn't so much the money as it was the waste. But she did look radiant when she put it on. *Radiant as she pushed me away yet another night.*

Out went the shoes and then he moved over to the cabinet that contained Sarah's hats. "I'm really going to enjoy getting rid of these monstrosities. They were her special love."

As he threw one of her larger hats out, the wind caught it and flung it up towards the sky. This particular hat had a very wide brim and with the air pumping it up, the top seemed pointed. "Behold, James. It certainly looks like witches 'apparel," yelled William as he exploded with an evil laugh.

Mr. Grady was manic. He continued to throw Sarah's possessions to the ground. James ran downstairs, grabbed some boxes and sacks from the pantry, ran out into the yard, and began to collect the clothes as fast as he could.

He had to duck sometimes as William's tosses were not always easy to navigate around. Now the aggrieved husband was in the bathroom throwing out bottles. James attempted to see that the glass containers did not hit the driveway and break. He wondered what William would try to do with the furniture in the sitting room because that all was considered Sarah's.

Eventually the liquor and some of the physical rage began to leave his body and William sat down on the floor in his upset bedroom, spent. He stayed like this for some time, mouth agape and stared at the ransacked closets.

Finally, he called out the window to James who was finishing collecting Sarah's belongings from the ground. "Come upstairs. I need you."

James put the last of Sarah's personal effects into a box and hustled upstairs. "What is it, Mr. Grady?"

"Where do you think she has gone? She wouldn't have run away with that ridiculous waiter turned car salesman. Most people loved Sarah, but she really only had one good friend. Do you think she went to June's house last night? Call the Johns residence."

Clearing his throat, James related what he thought would be best for William to hear. "Sir, Miss Sarah is gone. Mrs. Johns called this morning to see if we had any idea where she was. At your wife's request she did not attend the divorce trial yesterday and had no information until she saw the article in the morning paper saying Mrs. Grady had been arrested last night.

"Mrs. Johns took it upon herself to call Charles Bradley Motor Company to see if that salesman was still working. The company told her he didn't show up for work this morning. However, I find it difficult to believe that Miss Sarah would have gone away with that Charles Newlon or anyone else in town.

"Remember she had to have been terribly upset by the information that became public in the court proceedings. I'm sure no woman wants to be accused of many occurrences of adultery, especially when it can be proven. It's not only immoral; it's against the law."

James believed his relationship with Mr. Grady went somewhat beyond that of servant and employer, so he asked, "Do you want me to tell you what I think?" Without waiting for an answer, he continued, "You did the right thing by hiring that private detective to follow her for the last several months. You were also correct to divorce her; her lifestyle was out of control. But by making her actions public, you have destroyed her. She will never come back to Decatur."

"That's enough, James." But sad and sober, William whispered, "Where would she go? She's not on good terms with her family. With her son deceased she has no one except her friends and acquaintances in Decatur, and most of them are MY friends."

"She's alone and it serves her right. How could she humiliate me like she did? I will never be able to appear in public again either. James…she drove me to this!"

CHAPTER 3

The Monument

Evening May 18, 1921

After disposing of all of Sarah's possessions, William felt no better. By evening, he was sure she would not be coming home to collect her things any time soon, yet he longed for the satisfaction of seeing a humiliated wife come to him and beg for her things.

Although he had had only an hour of fitful sleep in the last two days, he was not tired. He tried to get a grip on reality, but the world seemed surreal. Rage still blazed inside him. What could rid him of his memories of Sarah?

He went outside to try to calm down and get some fresh air, not even noticing that James had picked up all the items he had tossed out the window. All he saw around the yard were her touches. Looking at the flowers growing everywhere, he couldn't help but appreciate her talent as a gardener. Sarah had gone to great lengths to get vines to grow up the sides of the house. It was the fashionable thing to do. But…now he hated those colorful reminders of her.

William annihilated the plants on one side of the house with ferocity. Looking down at the mess of vines on the ground, he realized he had hurt no one except the house and the yard, and still felt no better.

Where was she? William needed the gratification of seeing her feel pain. He needed to see the wild look she got in her eyes when things were not going right, the high voice she used when she hurt.

Sarah, he knew, would be suffering. She had been unaware of the fact that a private detective followed her for three months and had recorded all her transgressions. When these facts came out in the divorce trial, she had to have been blindsided by the depth of his knowledge. His only satisfaction in all of this.

William had deliberately left on the early train to Chicago the morning of the trial to avoid the proceedings with a manufactured business schedule. He did see one client in the city but the meeting was a disaster as he could not concentrate on what was being said. Having nothing to do to keep his mind off of the trial, he tried to keep busy in the Palmer House lobby with business proposals he had not as yet read.

He wanted the world to know he had real business to attend to and could not be bothered to sit through the court proceedings… but maybe that had been a mistake. He imagined her face as the detective rattled off times and places of her meetings with Charles Newlon, or whatever his name was. Her shame had to be apparent to everyone.

William wanted to see the same look reflected on her face as when Sam died, when she realized there were no more wars she could wage against the world to protect her son. But even that he wanted to take from her. How dare she mourn all this time as a Saint! All the while gallivanting like a common whore. *After all I did for her. That damned monument erected as a testament to a Mother's love. She called it her most cherished possession and visited the grave site daily. No, she no longer deserves to play the grieving mother. What could I do that would hurt her the most?*

In a flash it came to him. Sam's grave! This was the way to make her pay. He would destroy the monument! Having no visible reminder of Sam would deal the final blow to Sarah's psyche.

Do I need James 'help? No, I can do it myself. Besides James was fond of Sarah and probably would not approve of my actions. He didn't need trouble from James at this time. *Best not to involve him.* William planned to wait until it was dark.

Deciding that with the right tool he could accomplish the task alone, he went into the garage to look for the correct implement. James kept everything organized so it was easy to see what was there. The only problem was William didn't know a wrench from a hammer.

After looking the whole arsenal over, he grabbed the metal "thing" that he deemed to be the strongest. If he threw his weight behind it, he could accomplish the job.

When night came, he realized he had to drive the car to get to the cemetery. He was capable of driving but was not comfortable doing it. James took him where he wanted to go. But not tonight. James would remind him of the feelings he had for Sam, how he thought of him as a son, and would try to talk him out of wrecking Sam's monument.

Getting the car out of the garage was not as easy as William thought. He lurched forward instead of backward to begin. Luckily he didn't hit the back side of the garage, although he did bump into a barrel on the back wall. Never mind. Insignificant. He was in a hurry. As he went down the street, he wondered how he could speed up the drive. Every time he tried to go faster, he hit the curb on the side of the road. *These new cars were a lot harder to steer than a horse and buggy.*

While driving erratically to the cemetery, William congratulated himself on stumbling upon the one thing in Decatur that he was sure Sarah could not live without. Daily Sarah had paid tribute to her fallen son by placing a token at the base of his memorial. At the time, William had also been devastated by his death.

But now Sam is gone and, in reality, Sam was Sarah's from her first marriage, not mine. She never truly welcomed me into Sam's upbringing.

As he drove inside the cemetery, he was glad he knew exactly where the grave site was. It was too dark to see anything, even with the lights on the car. But that made conditions perfect for William to accomplish his mission. The nighttime sky was overcast. There was not a star in the heavens. The moon was hidden behind the clouds, so blackness engulfed the whole area. Luckily, William had thought to bring his large flashlight.

Even though he was only a mile away from his home on Millikin Place, civilization seemed far away. There were no houses near-by and the cemetery inhabitants all seemed happy in their own spaces. The stillness accentuated the serenity of the place making his surroundings seem peaceful. This was the antithesis of how William felt, so the quiet encouraged William's anger and he set about his business with a passion he had seldom experienced.

As he raised his weapon over his head, he caught the full view of the monument. The scene of he and Sarah discussing the memorial with an architect came rushing through his mind. Sarah would have built it to the sky. She wanted it bigger and bigger. Finally, William convinced her it would be more impressive to have it sculpted instead of just a huge pile of stone. They picked a beautiful red granite piece upon which an artist chiseled two doors that appeared to be opening. The doors on the finished piece were symbolic of Sam's entry to heaven. On one were the words "U. S. NAVAL PILOT Died September 1918" and on the other

"SAMUEL WEBSTER ELWOOD Born 1898". It stood as a gorgeous monument.

William's weapon crashed against the stone. A resounding "clang" vibrated through the entire area. William struck it again and again throwing his whole weight into each blow. "Clang, clang", but no progress was made. Not even a small scratch was visible on the beautiful granite sculpture. Why had they purchased such strong material? It was impenetrable.

William lost what little composure he had as he swung the steel bar over and over against the stone. His flashlight gave out on him. He took the cap off the top, removed the batteries, placed them back, and then tried to get it to light. No luck. He threw the cap off again and discovered that he had put the batteries in wrong. After resituating the batteries, it still would no longer light. He threw the flashlight as far as he could into the blackness and still pounded at the stone in the dark. Finally slumping down to the ground in front of the structure that defeated him, he sobbed…but only for a minute. Sitting up straight, he shouted to the sky, *"William Grady does not cry about things. I orchestrate them…I give the orders and people obey."*

Determining he needed to involve someone in his covert escapade that had a truck or a horse and wagon, he drove home to recruit James. The task was not one he could accomplish alone. He needed someone to remove the stone as a whole piece from the cemetery and dispose of it.

James had not yet retired to his room above the garage, because he was aware that William had taken the car. So when William drove into the garage, he was there to greet him. William immediately informed James of his next duty. "I don't want Sam's monument to remain in the cemetery. I want you to arrange to have it removed and destroyed…immediately."

Starting to object, James changed his mind as he looked at Mr. Grady's unemotional face. "If you're sure that's what you want, I'll take care of it right away."

"Great. I'll expect it to be gone by tomorrow."

James couldn't help informing his employer that what he was asking was against the law. "You know, if I would be caught taking away the stone, I would be arrested."

"It's my stone and I'll do what I wish with it," declared William as he went in the house. "And make up the bed in the guest room. Now!"

James muttered to himself as he put the clean sheets on the bed. "This should be Sadie's job, not mine." Sadie, who was Sarah's maid, had been fired by William the day before the divorce trial after eleven years of service to the Grady family.

William realized he could never sleep in the bed he had shared with Sarah ever again. As he crawled into the spare bed he scowled at the thought that even with her gone, he was left a guest in his own residence surrounded by her and her choices. Finally, the nothingness of sleep.

Hours later his eyes opened wide, instantly knowing the nightmare of this life was real. Numb, his thoughts turned to the room around him in the dim light of morning. All the guests welcomed to this room in their eighteen years together began to parade by in his mind.

His brother the priest had come to visit as often as he was allowed to get away from his parish. The brothers enjoyed their time together but always ended the visit with a conversation about William forsaking his Catholic religion. "William, you allow business to get in the way of your faith. Business has become your God."

The Rockafellows were guests from New York who spent many holidays with the Gradys. Ed, Florence, and their daughter Gwen always seemed to enjoy coming to Decatur. Ed was one of his long-time friends and also a business associate. William admired his intellect and his sense of what was right. Both business and social events always went better when Ed was a part of them.

William tried to think of other guests that had slept in this room that weren't closely aligned with Sarah. None came to mind, so he lay back down in the bed, not able to prepare himself for the misery of the day.

CHAPTER 4

Do Not Disturb

Decatur, Illinois May 19, 1921

James took care of the monument as promised. With his main job for the day addressed, he went about his business which now consisted mainly of answering the phone. Everyone was puzzled as to Sarah's whereabouts. June Johns, Sarah's best friend and confident, called to talk to James whom she knew adored Sarah.

"Have you heard from Sarah? Did she pick up any of her stuff from the house?" inquired June.

"No, Mrs. Johns. No one that I'm aware of has seen or heard from her," said James, feeling relieved that Mr. Grady had a private phone not a party line.

"I'm terribly worried about her. How could a well-dressed lady like Sarah in a bright blue Packard touring car just disappear? Well, I'm hiring a private detective to look for her," June announced.

"That's a good idea, Mrs. Johns," said James knowing it would be intense if an angry, enraged William found her first.

No sooner had James hung up the phone than Sarah's attorney, J. T. Whitley, called trying to find her. He said there were some unfinished details he needed to attend to, such as where to send her money from the settlement. Since William would not speak to anyone, James simply told him they had no clue where Sarah was.

James continued his daily tasks staying as close to the phone as he could.

"Mr. Grady is not taking calls at the moment... No, I don't know when he'll be able to return your call. I'll give him your message."

Deciding Mr. Grady had had enough sleep, James went upstairs in the afternoon and knocked on the guestroom door. But there was no answer. After knocking several more times, he became a bit alarmed and opened the door. William was awake, sitting up in the bed, staring at the closed curtains. Without turning his head to acknowledge James' presence, he growled, "What do you want?"

"I thought you might want to come downstairs and eat some breakfast. It's two-thirty in the afternoon," said James. "Also your office called and asked that you call them back today. Sarah's attorney would like you to contact him. Mr. Irving called, Mr. Bering wanted to talk to you, and..."

"Stop! I told you I won't speak to anyone right now," barked William. "Leave me alone! You handle things. All I want is to be sure Sam's monument disappears."

"I took care of that. It's gone," said a frustrated James.

CHAPTER 5

The Getaway

Decatur, Illinois Evening May 18, 1921

Arrested! I'll never live this down. I've got to get away… I can't breathe!

Sarah Grady pressed harder on the accelerator as she strained to calm her racing heart. No moon lit the sky…just total darkness except for the headlights on her Packard. How long would those last? How far could she drive at this hour on this bumpy road?

Trying to decide where to go took more concentration than she could muster. *I need some sleep.* In addition to the horrible degrading divorce proceeding this morning, she had been arrested a few hours ago. Hardly recalling the actual arrest, she remembered only her release from the judge after paying a fine. *It's all William's fault. I have to get away. If he finds me, he'll be full of wrath.* The many drinks consumed to get her through the day were taking their toll. *I should never have drunk so many gin and tonics. I can no longer think.*

Her stomach tightened every time the car lurched into a hole in the road. But so far her big expensive touring car managed to keep going. By fleeing from Decatur, she realized she alone was taking charge of her life. Maybe her decisions so far had been hasty because she had nothing with her: no clothes, no money, no furniture, nothing but the outfit she was wearing and her car. She had the presence of mind to stop by her house and try to get some clothes, but William had made that impossible by stationing two policemen in the house with instructions not to let Sarah in. William's word was law in Decatur. Not that all this mattered, because now life as she knew it would not include William. Still she had the feeling she needed to hide from him…disappear.

During the war she often had traveled the roads alone for the Red Cross to different cities in central Illinois, but not at 2:00 AM when it was pitch black outside and prime time for marauders to be out on the road.

Sarah Grady, pull over to the side of the road and rest. In the morning if someone hasn't killed you, you can drive on to …oh, maybe Bloomington.

She pulled off the road, shut off her car and began to sob. After several minutes, she brushed the tears from her eyes, covered herself with the lush blue lap robe that was kept in the car, laid her head back on the luxurious upholstery, and closed her eyes. Immediately she was in a sound sleep.

The bright sunlight of early morning slanted through the Packard's window. Opening her eyes, Sarah was confronted by the rat-a-tat-tat of a woodpecker chipping away at a nearby tree. Her head was throbbing and her mind was foggy. *Where am I? Oh yes, I remember now. My soon-to-be ex-husband had me locked out of my house (his house now) after he disgraced me in the divorce court proceedings. He was in Chicago during the trial not even having the courage to face me. He had me arrested!*

I have to find a new home…can't go back to Decatur. William is unstable. Mad. In her mind Sarah relived the events of yesterday. She remembered trying to pull herself together in Charles's apartment when she vowed to quit drinking. Then Charles came home, and, in spite of her good intentions, they began to party and make love. William's private detective followed their every move and gave the police an account of their activities so they could be arrested. *I forget the charge…no, I remember. It was disorderly conduct.*

Sarah maneuvered her car back onto the road and continued the drive towards Bloomington. Arriving without incident before noon, she stopped at a telegraph office to have money wired to a local bank. Thank goodness she had taken care before the divorce proceedings to see that her money would be readily available to her. *It is my money after all.* Thanks to her father, her first husband, and Ed Rockafellow, she had a fortune of her own.

"Where would you suggest I eat lunch?" Sarah asked of the telegraph operator. "And do you know of a really nice rooming house where I could spend the night?"

Eyeing Sarah suspiciously, the operator told her to eat at the restaurant two doors north of the telegraph office, Aunt Emma's Eatery, and a block further to the north was the nicest rooming house in town, Tilly's Rooms for Hire. The information she needed was accompanied by a stern warning. "Miss, you best be careful wandering around by yourself, and if you carry some of that money you wired for, it could be dangerous."

"Thanks for the warning, but I know how to take care of myself. I've done it all my life."

After picking up her money at the bank, Sarah went to Aunt Emma's Eatery and had a substantial lunch. Not having had a meal since breakfast the previous day, she quickly rediscovered her appetite.

Next she visited three ladies 'dress shops and bought some clothes. The dresses she purchased were not the quality she was accustomed to. "Do you have anything that comes from Paris for this season?" she would ask hopefully in each store, but the answer, as she suspected, was always "no". Her purchase from a nearby leather shop provided a trunk to keep the new clothes in. *Well, these are everyday house clothes but at least they will appear clean.*

At last she pulled her car up in front of the rooming house the telegraph operator recommended and knocked on the door hoping she looked like a normal traveler. She had never had any experience with this type of establishment before.

"I would like a room for two nights," said Sarah to the plump, smiling woman who answered the door. "You must be Tilly."

The landlady quickly sized Sarah up and said, "Yes, I'm Tilly and I have a nice room for you. Come in, honey."

The house was an old Victorian complete with all the clutter that Sarah spent so much time removing from her previous homes. Dodging a grandfather clock, a large chest, two marble tables, and an overstuffed chair covered in a velvet crimson material, she followed Tilly through the small reception hall.

Arriving in the parlor, Tilly sat at a desk loaded with stacks of papers and began to register Sarah for her room. "Name, please."

Sarah tensed. *Did she want anyone to know what her real name was? What if William was still so angry that he came looking for her? Maybe the paper in Bloomington would pick up the story of my arrest from Decatur. Tilly probably would not be happy having a criminal in her house.*

"Name, please," Tilly repeated.

"Uh, Sadie Elwood," lied Sarah. She reasoned that Elwood had been her name when she was married to her first husband and "Sadie" was the name on her birth certificate which William suggested she change to Sarah.

"Address?"

Oh, these questions are so difficult to answer. "I no longer have an address as I'm in the process of moving to…(*where, Sarah?*)…to Chicago."

Having run a rooming house for many years, Tilly knew when clients were not being fully honest with her and decided not to ask any more questions. She asked for two nights deposits up front and proceeded to make Sarah comfortable in one of the rooms upstairs.

"Herman will bring up your trunk and supper will be at six o'clock."

Momentarily forgetting the circumstances of where she was, she asked, "Will it be alright if I don't dress for dinner? I didn't bring many clothes with me."

Tilly seemed to be confused by the question, but told Sarah that she could wear anything she wished to dinner.

Settling into her room gave Sarah the relief she needed to relax and begin thinking about her past indiscretions and what she wanted to do with the future. *Where should I go to start a new chapter in my life?*

CHAPTER 6

Decisions

Bloomington, Illinois May 20, 1921

Sarah spent a day and two nights in the rooming house trying to piece herself back together. Sitting on a wicker chair across the room from the big mirror on the burled walnut dresser, she stared at herself through the freckled glass. She acknowledged her indiscretions: her love affair with Ed Rockafellow, the drinking, the idiotic fling with Charles, and her refusal to obey William's dictates.

Never would she return to Decatur. Not only did she fear William, but also she had been publicly denigrated. Her country club friends would no longer accept her. Not that they ever fully did. *My so-called friends have always seemed jealous of me. I'm sure they are ecstatic about my divorce and arrest, and they have a right to be. I'm so ashamed. Except for June, I have nothing left in Decatur besides my son's grave. Maybe I could sneak back to Decatur someday to visit June and Sam's grave.* She couldn't bear the thought of never bringing flowers to Sam's place of rest again.

Sarah had visited her son's grave every day rain or shine. Three years ago during the war, Sam Elwood, her son by her first husband, caught the Spanish flu and died in a navy hospital in Chelsea, Massachusetts.

Her grief and guilt were palpable. Her grief was normal for a mother, but, in addition, she carried overwhelming guilt for having left him in the custody of her first husband's mother as he grew up.

When Sarah divorced her unfaithful first husband, she couldn't take Sam with her until she found a suitable home for the two of them. He seemed better off with Grandmother Elwood. Then she met William in Chicago and they married. As she was about to bring Sam to the big city, Faries Manufacturing transferred William to Decatur. At that point William needed Sarah to entertain his clients and she was too busy to spend much time with Sam.

It was only in the last few years of his life that Sam stayed with Sarah and William. Sarah missed most of his childhood and never forgave herself for that.

How to deal with Sam now would be a problem that Sarah wondered if she could solve by having his body reburied in Colo, Iowa where his Grandmother lived. Sam's father and grandmother both would be happy and she could visit his grave any time she wished. *Yes, Sam would be with people he loved. I could ask Grandmother Elwood to handle the details so I wouldn't have to be involved in the move. That would solve the problem.*

Sarah had spent the last two days giving herself pep talks. *I am a strong woman, not because of William, but in spite of him. He held me back from becoming an even stronger person and accomplishing most of what I wanted to do.*

I don't want to see any of the people I knew in my past life. I'll be careful in crafting my new one so history does not repeat itself. I am so ashamed and humiliated for having acted the way I did. How does someone who worked as hard as I did for Prohibition become an alcoholic?

I want no one to even know that I'm alive...not William, not my family, not even Ed. I wanted to see him so badly the night I left Decatur that's why I wrote that letter to him hoping he would come to our special place and I could be with him. I wish I had not been so weak. I need to have a new beginning which cannot include Ed. I find it difficult to think of my soulmate as a mistake, but I was wrong to be unfaithful to my husband for four years. I won't show up at our special place and Ed won't think I am still alive. Maybe that way I can really have a new start.

Where do I go to disappear? Dixon, Illinois might be good. I have property there. No... It's too small a town. I guess I really don't have much choice. I'll have to go to Chicago. Even if people look for me there, no one will find me. I can hide. I'm glad of it. Good riddance, Mrs. W. J. Grady.

As Sarah checked out, she thanked Tilly for her hospitality and asked her to forget that she was ever there. Tilly smiled as she wondered how she could forget that a lady in the most expensive car she had ever seen came knocking on her door alone, paying in advance for two nights and never leaving the room except for an occasional meal.

"I'll keep your secret, honey, whatever it is," said Tilly.

Sarah simply said, "Thank you."

Hopping into her car Sarah began to feel like a new adventure awaited her, an exciting one. Chicago as a destination seemed like a wise choice. She would be able to sell her car there and find an apartment to live in where she would never be located by William or her old friends and acquaintances.

I'm forty-three years old. I just read that life expectancy for women is forty-seven, so I should at least have four more good years.

Sarah eased into the driver's seat of the blue Packard with the car pointed north. As she sat there, Carl Sandburg's poem "Chicago" popped into her head. "Hog Butcher of the world…So proud to be alive." She had made the right decision .No more regrets. She was free, headed for the big city and yes… so proud to be alive.

CHAPTER 7

---★---

A New Life

Chicago, Illinois May 21, 1921

Sarah made herself comfortable behind the steering wheel of the blue Packard. The early morning sun threw its bright rays down to glitter on the shiny metal of the touring car creating a spectacular light show. She couldn't help but smile at the beautiful sight.

Driving towards Chicago and her new life, she reflected that the only material thing from her past life that she really loved was this beautiful car. Having lived in Chicago when she and William were married, she was familiar with the great public transportation system in the city and realized the car might be a determent rather than an asset. She didn't want to sell the lovely Packard, but this was going to be a new life.

Sarah wished to prove to herself how powerful her internal strength was. So, while driving, she removed the long pins holding the large wide-brimmed hat on her head and, in an act of great defiance, placed the hat on the seat beside her. Never had she been out in public without a hat on her head. She felt new.

Outside of a few rather large holes in the road, the actual drive to the big city was long but uneventful. It was almost dinner time when Sarah began to see the outline of some of Chicago's taller buildings.

Passing by a large railroad yard which told her she was not too far from the inner city, she tried to decide where to stay…temporarily. *I need a hotel room, but not one of the nice places where travelers I know from Decatur would stay. If I can find a hotel on the outskirts of downtown, I will be safe. No one must know where I am.*

About two miles from the center of town, as if in answer to Sarah's criteria, a rather pleasant looking hotel appeared. Upon investigation she found the establishment had a nice restaurant and would take care of her car. *This will keep me well settled for the moment.*

As the bell-hop ushered her into the room, Sarah noticed a well-dressed woman entering the room across the hall. The woman stared intensely at her, but not in an unfriendly way. The woman nodded her head in greeting before entering her room. Strangely Sarah felt an affinity toward her.

Sarah tipped the bell-hop and surveyed the room with her knowledgeable eye. It wasn't the Palmer House or Edgewater Beach but cleanliness obviously ruled. It was sparsely furnished although all the necessities were there. She bounced on the bed and decided the hotel would do at least for a day or two.

She lay down on the bed without unpacking and immediately fell asleep. Exhausted from the long drive from Bloomington she did not wake up till eight o'clock the next morning. That was a late hour for Sarah to begin her day, but she reasoned this was a new life. Yes, for real, this was a new life. No longer did she have to get up at 5:45 and start on the tasks William had laid out for her. Dressing in some of her new unfashionable clothes purchased in Bloomington, she went downstairs to have breakfast.

The hotel restaurant had only two occupied tables. The well-dressed woman Sarah had seen across the hall last night was dining alone at one table. *It would be nice to talk to someone and she's obviously by herself.*

She looks like a nice respectable person. I think I'll risk asking to sit with her.

"Excuse me. I saw you last night in the hallway as I was arriving. I'm alone. Would it be acceptable for me at sit at your table?" asked Sarah.

The woman smiled and said, "Of course. I was going to ask you when I determined whether or not you were by yourself. Please sit down. I'm Elizabeth Parker."

Sarah stiffened a bit as she realized she had to give a name. *I guess I'll just be Sadie for now.* "My name is Sadie Elwood."

The women ordered their breakfast then spent a few minutes in meaningless chatter as they sized up each other. By the time the food arrived they had begun to enjoy each other's company.

The ladies chatted for another few minutes until Elizabeth confessed, "My husband is divorcing me. He threw me out of the house only allowing me to pack a few clothes."

"We have some things in common then," said Sarah. "I have been removed from my house and my marriage, but you were luckier than I. My husband would not even allow me to gather one article of clothing."

Not wanting to go further into the details of her break up with a stranger, Elizabeth rose from the table saying, "Let's get together for lunch sometime soon so we can share our stories."

"I'd be delighted to do just that."

Sarah went back to her room and sat on the edge of her bed. *Here I am. What do I do now with my new life? I have a good mind for business. Maybe I could start one of my own.* Reviewing in her mind what her experiences had been with her first husband's real estate and land businesses, with William's large corporation, and even with Ed's company, she realized she was qualified in many different capacities.

Yes, I will start a business. Something I would enjoy working at. Money is not a problem. First, I'd better find a place to live where I will be comfortable and no one can trace me.

Sarah got ready to leave her room to go find an apartment. Looking around the room she discovered that she only had two hats, the one she left Decatur in and one that she bought in Bloomington, neither of which she thought appropriate for her current trip.

I know what I can do. I'll open a hat shop.

Having made a decision she bounced down the stairs, not waiting for the elevator.

Coming into the lobby, she witnessed a tearful Elizabeth standing at the front desk. The hotel clerk was talking to her with his voice raised. People in the lobby were beginning to stop and try to see what was going on.

Immediately Sarah went over to find out what the problem was. "Elizabeth, what is wrong?"

"They think I am trying to scam them by not paying my bill. I have never been so humiliated. I was so upset when I left home that I didn't bring much cash with me. I told them I could go to a bank and get the money I owe them, but they said I couldn't leave until the police get here."

Sarah turned to face the clerk. "Shame on you. Do you know who this is? This woman has never scammed anyone in her entire life. How much money does she owe you?"

"She owes for the night's room and her breakfast which is $10.00," said the agitated clerk firmly.

Sarah placed a ten dollar bill on the counter. "If you can stop the police from coming do so now. Otherwise when they get here, I'll tell them I am going to sue you for libel."

The flustered clerk already was on the phone to stop the police from coming.

"Come on, Elizabeth. Let's go find a place to sit and have a cup of coffee."

Elizabeth was happy just to be led by Sarah. Next to the hotel was a small little restaurant that looked friendly.

They sat in a booth and Elizabeth looked at Sarah with tearful eyes. "How can I thank you. I guess I'm not used to handling situations by myself. This divorce thing is new. I forgot to get my money from the bank. Until our divorce becomes final, I may have trouble getting cash, but I will pay you back this afternoon.

"Don't worry about that. You can pay me back when it's convenient. Maybe if you talk about your husband it will help you deal with the trauma. Why did your husband throw you out?

"That's an easy question to answer. He could no longer abide my quest for independence. After this morning, I wonder if I really want to be as independent as I thought."

Elizabeth's eyes began to tear as she attempted to give Sarah a rather flippant reply to her question. Pretending not to see the tears, Sarah encouraged her to tell her story.

Elizabeth took a handkerchief out of her pocketbook and wiped her eyes. "Thank you, Sadie. I didn't realize how badly I needed to talk to someone until you sat down with me. I have many people who now call me 'friend'… but will no longer when I'm not Richard Parker's wife."

Sarah quickly responded, "I understand. For fifteen years I have been Mrs. William J. Grady and according to our newspaper 'number one society lady'. I destroyed that myth when I was divorced from William and became only Sarah Grady. The country club ladies that I have known for years don't know Sarah Grady. I have only one friend left. Please go on with your story."

Sarah realized she had just given Elizabeth her real name, but as she looked at her new friend she was not concerned. Elizabeth was too wrapped up in her own troubles to notice.

Elizabeth continued, "We seem to have much in common. For eighteen years I was a weak person and did what I was told by my husband. Finally, I recognized I wasn't really living and decided to try some things I had on MY 'to do' list. All I really wanted was to have the freedom to join an organization of my own choosing, to maybe redecorate a room with furniture and colors that I like, to make the weekly menu for the cook…"

Sarah interrupted, "Oh really! You couldn't even have the food you wanted? You were as regulated as I was."

Elizabeth shook her head and paused to take a small sip from her cup before she continued, "Well, I finally decided to just walk away. When I told him, he didn't seem very upset. He only mused about the dinner he was giving next Wednesday and who would host it with him.

I'm sure he will try to get by without paying me any money in the divorce, but I think I have enough of my own to get by. I'm forty-three years old and I'd like to live for a while!"

The ladies talked for over an hour and discovered they had much in common including looking for a place to call home in Chicago. Both felt like they had found a 'friend' and left the restaurant excited to go house-hunting together to find themselves a place to call home.

CHAPTER 8

Sarah Settles In

Chicago, Illinois May 30, 1921

The building manager opened the heavy rather luxurious looking wooden door so Sarah and Elizabeth could enter the apartment. This was the third place they had looked at and they were beginning to get a little discouraged. Sarah walked across the room spying two large ceiling to floor windows.

"Oh, Elizabeth, look at that view of the garden out of the living room windows. I like this place already," said Sarah.

"This room is good sized and has space at one end for dining…and look two big bedrooms and a bath over here," said Elizabeth as she moved swiftly around the whole apartment.

After discovering a small sun room with a bay window that would be perfect for her office, Sarah smiled as she took her time going over the entire apartment. The quarter-sawn oak on one wall defining the dining area had just the right tone. The wallpaper in the bedroom had robins sitting on the branches of a cherry tree. So homey. She felt peaceful. This would be her new home.

"Are you two ladies thinking of taking an apartment together? If not, I have another space just like this across the hall," said the manager.

Sarah, forever the business woman, began to ask the practical questions…How much is the monthly rent, what about the utilities, etc. Having decided ahead of time that they each would live in their own place, Sarah said she would sign a lease for the apartment. Elizabeth followed saying the same for the space across the hall.

"This is ideal, Sadie. We will be living close but not together. Perfect place," said Elizabeth.

Sarah's Apartment Building

The hotel that held Sarah's apartment was not new. In the beginning it only had single rooms, but in 1918 the owners remodeled it into an extended-stay featuring attractive apartments. Sarah felt content knowing she was moving into a fashionable apartment. She was accustomed to having luxuries. Also, it was on the corner of Hollywood and Kenmore, an upscale neighborhood, but away from the downtown places that Decatur people would be frequenting.

It took her only five days to gather enough of the necessities to be able to move into her new quarters. After placing all the newly purchased furniture, she looked around nodding her head in approval. The lamp and table she had just purchased reminded her of furniture she and William had bought in California when they were first married, only this time she alone selected it. Sarah felt she had done a good job picking out the apartment and was happy to have her new friend across the hall.

Settling herself in the new freshly installed leisure chair with its silky smooth beige covering, she drifted between sleep and wakefulness as she picked the thoughts she wanted to consume her. The negative thoughts won first place as she mulled over her regrets.

I regret Ed wasn't ready to leave his wife so we could be together. I regret drinking alcohol to end my aching for Ed and also losing my morality with Charles. I regret writing that letter to Ed when I left Decatur. That chapter in my life is over. I regret that I haven't gotten in touch with June. She probably thinks I'm dead.

Next Sarah's mind went to William. Knowing that he was humiliated, she believed that he wanted revenge for what she did to him.

He scares me. I was grieving because Ed was no longer in my life, but I treated my husband badly. I know. To make up for my bad behavior, I'll make a will and leave everything to him. Money to buy the presidency of Faries Manufacturing is all he really cares about.

I am Sarah Peterson Elwood Grady. I refuse to give over to my negatives. I am beginning a new life and I will be happy. Slowly she drifted into a peaceful sleep.

CHAPTER 9

Hope

Hot Springs, Virginia May 30 1921

Ed Rockafellow sat alone at a dining room table in the Hot Springs Resort. A handsome man in his fifties, the picture of propriety. When the waiter approached, he said. "I'm so sorry to keep you running to my table just to get me another ginger ale. I'll be ready to order dinner soon, but right now please bring me another ginger ale. Thank you for such great service."

He really had no appetite for food only wishing to absorb the atmosphere around him. This was where they met. It was here at this resort that they fell in love, danced, walked in the garden, and played golf. At every glance around the dining room he found a memory of his beloved Sarah.

He reached his fingers into his watch pocket and slowly pulled out a folded, dog-eared piece of paper. He stared for a moment at the wadded letter and then carefully unfolded it.

A week ago he had received the correspondence from Sarah Grady whom he hadn't seen or heard from for almost two years. When she terminated their affair, she had dictated that he was not to write or call her ever again. Ed had been totally devastated, but respected her wishes. And then this letter.

Sarah was his soul mate, his only love. He had never understood why she had stepped away from him. They were making plans to get married after they both divorced and each of them was contributing monthly to a mutual stock account to save for their future.

Sitting forward in the dining chair, he again read the note Sarah had sent him on May 18th.

My Darling Soul Mate,

Forgive me, my love. I have broken so many oaths to you which we once made with such soul-binding fervor. As you can surmise from the papers on which I write to you, in your absence I have torn away all that I am, all that was once your Sallie. On this night, as I answer for all that I've done and dare to contemplate what I shall do, I think of you, and must have you know that I vow to be the woman you saw in me once more. Tomorrow I will claim the few things I need in this world and then go to our special place. I pray God will restore me and perhaps even restore our love.

Forever! I do. Do you?

Since the note was written on a paper from her divorce proceedings, he could infer she was now a free woman, but still couldn't understand why she wrote to him. Did she still love him? She referred to their special place which had to be Hot Springs. So for the last few days he had been at the resort hoping that she would show up.

However, after also receiving a note from Sarah's best friend June stating she feared for Sarah's safety, along with the newspaper article describing Sarah's arrest, Ed shared June's fears that something terrible had happened to Sarah. He suspected Sarah had been overwhelmed by grief and remorse. Probably didn't know which way to turn. If only he had been there to help her through this trying time.

When he left home he told his wife that he had to meet a business friend at the resort. Florence was upset as usual because she had plans for him to take her to the theater.

Ed replayed the scene in his mind:

"Everyone I know will be at the new musical Friday night. The Schubert is showing 'Hello Dolly'. If we don't go, I will be left out of conversations and our group will wonder why we weren't there. Surely you can wait and go to Virginia on Saturday?" said a frustrated Florence.

"I'm sorry. Can't we go see the play when I return," said Ed knowing that it wasn't the theater in which she feigned interest, but only her social group. "How about I take you to Ellen's before I go to the station?"

Florence sighed and stood still a moment, then said, "I'm sure you don't have time to take me anywhere."

"Florence, I bought you a car because you said you wanted to able to go where and when you wanted," said Ed. "I'm sorry, but I really do need to go catch my train."

Ed tried to leave his wife in a good mood, but realized he could not be successful. Taking more time with her wouldn't help his marital situation and right then all he could think of was Sarah.

Now here he was at the special place that he and Sarah had shared so often waiting and hoping against hope that she would appear.

The patient waiter swung by Ed's table again. "Could I get you some dinner, Mr. Rockafellow?"

Ed willed himself back to the moment and simply shook his head no. He started to realize that his beloved Sarah was not going to show up. Allowing himself to dream for a few minutes, he conjured up an image of Sarah as she was in this dining room two years ago…his true love. How beautiful she appeared then.

He crumpled the letter and placed it on the table, rising to leave, knowing he would not see her. He stood by his table for a minute then picked up the letter again and left the dining room.

Ed caught the next train back to New York vowing he would try to think of something nice to do for Florence when he returned. But all the way home he dreamed of his soul mate Sarah with an uneasiness he couldn't shake. He worried that something horrible had happened to her. If only I could help her.

CHAPTER 10

⸻ ★ ⸻

The Recluse

Summer 1921

June, July, and August passed and William would not interrelate with people or events. No matter who called on the phone or came to the house in person, they were not allowed to see or talk to him. He seldom shaved and James had to insist occasionally that he change his clothes.

James did his best, but was overwhelmed. He used all his charm to talk Mrs. Chambers the cook into staying. He went to the store to get groceries and she came in the afternoon to cook dinner which James served in style in the dining room.

To keep the household running, James ran up bills all over town. Luckily, Mr. Grady's credit was stellar. At the end of the month, William would write a note to the bank directing them to take care of his debts and someone there would pay all the bills from his account.

One day, sitting in his now normal place in the big upholstered chair in the library, William confided to James. "My life is over. I have been so thoroughly humiliated by my wife… ex-wife… that I don't wish to face my friends and business associates." After thinking a moment he said "Maybe I could move to California and start all over."

That wouldn't do. Everywhere I look I would see Sarah and the good times we had there. I need closure. I need to see Sarah. She's done this to me. After everything I've done for her, I'm the one suffering.

As always James just sighed and said, "Yes, Mr. Grady."

No one knew where Sarah was. She had completely disappeared. William was left bereft and unsatisfied. Externally his rage had subsided to dull detachment, but inside his fervor burned.

One day on a beautiful, sunny, early fall evening while William was picking at his supper in the dining room, James allowed Mr. Irving from next door to come in the back door and go talk to William. Mr. Irving was not only president of Faries Manufacturing, but was also his neighbor and a good friend.

Mr. Irving pulled up a chair and began to scold William. "I know you don't want to talk to me, but I want to talk to you. Do you realize it has been three and a half months since your divorce trial?"

William continued eating his dinner without changing his sour expression.

"It's time you came back into the world. Your friends understand what a terrible experience you have been through and are anxious to help you recover. Faries Manufacturing needs you; after all, you are an officer of the company. Your golf team needs you. All your organizations need you."

William's expression hardened and he began chasing his peas around in a circle on his plate with his fork, but still said nothing.

Mr. Irving had had enough, he roared at his friend, "Stop acting like a two year old and be a man."

William put down his fork and met Mr. Irving's eye.

Clearing his throat, Mr. Irving continued in a calmer tone, "Start out by joining the golf tournament at the Country Club in two weeks. Don't leave your team short a person. Let me tell them you'll be there. Don't just sit here in your house decaying. The shame is not yours, Bill."

William's face softened. "Fine…you're right. Tell the club I'll play."

When Mr. Irving left, William sat in the dining room not really thinking about what his visitor had said, but pondering why all his friends called him "Bill" and Sarah fondly always called him "William".

For the two weeks between Mr. Irving's visit and the golf tournament, William tried each day to contemplate returning to the world of Decatur, Illinois. James helped promote the idea of him supporting his golf team and even got him to go once to the course to practice.

The day of the tournament dawned as a bright sunny day, warm but not hot. William was terrified of his return to normal social activities. *I can't use the weather as an excuse not to play.* James drove William to the course and handed the golf clubs to the young boy who was to caddy for William that day. William's negative attitude spilled over into everybody and everything. *I don't think I like this caddy.* William went through the motions of warming up. As he began to swing the golf clubs he felt …good. *Okay, I'll go through with this.* Feeling a little like a real person again, he decided if he was to play, he would play to win.

On hole number five he struggled because that was Sarah's favorite and in his mind he could see her shots take form. He knew just where most of her balls would go. Teeing up he stood facing the ball. *Why am I nervous? I know I can hit the ball farther than Sarah used to.* He swung his club as hard as he could and followed it into the air with his eyes. Noting the ball did not go as high into the air as usual, he breathed a big sigh of relief when his drive finally landed just a little further than Sarah's used to. But he did not finish the hole satisfactorily.

Hole after hole his aim was only to outplay her. Even when his team was handed the tournament trophy, he looked back at the course seeing the ghost of her wiry smile and jests at his play.

"Great to have you back, Bill."

"Real nice game, Bill"

"Beautiful shot on number eight."

His friends were happy to see him and struggled to act naturally. Everyone sensed it was a difficult thing for him to act like nothing had happened, but they all tried to ignore the past.

William appreciated what his friends attempted to do to make him feel normal, but he wasn't normal.

Angry and empty, he returned home. He concluded he could not face the world. Home was the best place for him to be.

CHAPTER 11

The Business Woman Emerges

Chicago, Illinois June 1921

A week after moving in Sarah considered herself settled. She called Elizabeth to come over and hear her plans.

"Thanks for coming. Are you settled in yet?" asked Sarah.

"Yes, but not like you. You make decisions faster than anyone I know," answered Elizabeth.

"I guess I do tend to make up my mind quickly. Like now. I have decided to open a millinery shop. Would you like to be partners with me?"

"Oh, Sadie, I don't know anything about business," said an astounded Elizabeth.

"Just come along as I put the essentials in place. You can decide later whether or not you want to be part of this."

With Elizabeth trailing along, Sarah quickly found a building she felt would be ideal for her hat shop.

"Location is very important," Sarah informed Elizabeth. "This building is close to our neighborhood. The ladies living nearby all need hats and they can easily walk to our door."

A reluctant Elizabeth noted, "But my husband said we are in a deep depression right now. Will ladies still come to buy hats?"

"Of course they will. This depression is almost over. The country seems to be recovering and we will take advantage of that."

The next day Sarah phoned all the suppliers that she was aware of in New York and wired money for them to begin shipping merchandise. Having purchased many hats on her own from a designer in Paris, she called upon his shop, La Plume, to send several of their creations for her planned opening next month.

"Now all we have to do is get the building ready and start a marketing campaign," said Sarah.

Elizabeth expressed her astonishment with the speed at which Sarah was moving and said she would be excited to be a partner in the shop, "But first I will have to ask Madame Lily if I have made the right decision."

"Madame Lily? An astrologer? Do you believe in the stars?" asked Sarah.

"The stars have ruled my life. Madame Lily foretold that I was marrying the wrong man. She was right when she told me I was going to have a miscarriage and would never have children. Not long ago she told me I would soon be out on my own. She has been right at every turn so I need to go see her now," said Elizabeth.

"I have a friend, June, who also believes in astrology. I guess she asked about me in one of her sessions with her Madame and some of my problems were predicted," said Sarah. "I believe that was a lucky guess on her Madame's part. Sorry, I think its mumbo jumbo, but entertaining. I should go with you and maybe learn of my future."

"It's in the stars," chirped Elizabeth.

Sarah did go with Elizabeth to see Madame Lily. They were ushered into a room that had red and black drapes hung all over the walls and ceiling. Sitting at a table with a crystal ball in the center was a middle aged woman with a turban on her head and lots of big, gaudy jewelry around her neck and on her fingers. The whole setting including the woman looked fraudulent to Sarah. *How could Elizabeth be taken in by her?*

However, Sarah was soon amazed at how much the self-proclaimed clairvoyant knew about events in her past. Things that she had never told Elizabeth. Madame Lily saw Sam's death, she saw her break-up with Ed, and she saw the divorce. Sarah was startled that so much of her life seemed to be an open book to this woman. So when Madame Lily told her she was going to have a successful business, she, as well as Elizabeth, became a believer.

"Madame Lily says it's a go, so I'm all in as a partner. I might be able to contribute because I design and make hats," said Elizabeth.

"I noticed the one you had on yesterday and intended to ask where you got it. Did you design that one?" inquired Sarah.

"Yes, I did. I make all my hats."

"You're very talented. Let me know what you need and you can start supplying our shop," said Sarah while hugging her new partner.

Within a month Sarah and Elizabeth had remodeled their building and had a fair amount of merchandise in stock. Sarah began an advertising campaign touting the grand opening of S & E Hats.

The ladies worked well together and fashioned a fantastic shop. On their opening day a line of well dressed women formed down the street for almost a block waiting for the door to open. When they unlocked the door the crowd flooded in. Success! Sarah knew her marketing campaign had worked.

"Let's hope our success continues. Wouldn't it be wonderful if we could make money doing something we love," said Sarah as Elizabeth nodded her head.

Surveying her new shop Sarah couldn't help but think of William. He would be critical of her efforts, and her achievement would feed his anger to a dangerous degree.

I've got to sell my car before William is able to trace it and find me. Maybe I'm wrong and he doesn't care where or if I am, but I don't want to take any chances.

CHAPTER 12

The Truth

Chicago, Illinois June 1921

"Elizabeth, I'll be downstairs waiting for you," yelled Sarah opening the door of her partner's apartment enough to be heard. They were going to their shop on a Sunday morning to make some changes that were not possible when customers were there.

"See you in a few minutes," shouted Elizabeth from her bedroom.

Sarah tripped lightly down the wide staircase enjoying the fact that she felt relaxed and happy. She had a shop that was well on its way to becoming very successful and no male in her life to make it difficult. As she reached the first floor she bumped into a man wandering around the room. Instinctively he put out his hand to steady her.

While still holding on to her arm, the man apologized, "So sorry, Miss. I didn't mean to run into you, but now that I have I can't say that I'm regretful. Anytime you can stop and chat with a beautiful woman ..."

All her life Sarah had been confronted by men. Undaunted by his seductive smile, Sarah placed the man in a category she knew so well "flirty womanizer". She decided to play the game. "Sir, I most certainly forgive you. It was your strong arm that prevented my fall."

"Please come. Sit down in a chair until you catch your breath. By the way my name is Richard Parker."

Sarah had to bite her lip to keep from laughing out aloud. Here she was, being flirted with by Elizabeth's soon to be ex-husband. Maybe she could make Elizabeth's divorce easier on her by showing off the character of this man.

"Were you coming to visit someone here in the apartment house?"

"Well, yes but that's not important now. Can I make up for my clumsiness by taking you out to brunch? And may I ask your name?"

As Sarah tried to decide what to do next, Elizabeth came down the stairs. "Sadie, I see you have met my soon-to-be ex-husband."

"Yes. Richard just asked me out for brunch." Sarah turned to Richard and asked, "I assume that the invitation includes your wife...soon-to- be your ex."

Richard turned red and began to mutter, "Well, I bumped into...I came to get you to sign some stuff...I didn't know you were friends."

Elizabeth said in a strong voice, "I'm busy right now, but stop in our shop sometime and I will look at your papers. It's the S & E Hat Shop about three blocks down on Hollywood."

Richard mumbled something and practically ran out of the building.

"Elizabeth, I hope you don't mind but I thought I would play along with him to show you what kind of a man you are divorcing," said Sarah.

"To see him flustered and caught in the act, so to speak, was wonderful. Thank you for letting me see in person what he is like," replied Elizabeth.

Sarah had had fun with Richard but now she realized she really needed to tell Elizabeth her real name and give her the details of her former life. Elizabeth was already curious why Sarah wanted to take her car to

Madison to sell it. .And Sarah thought it was only a matter of time until she slipped up and Elizabeth saw some papers dealing with her properties that were in the name of Sarah Grady.

"Let me take you out to brunch at the Palmer House after we're done working. I have some things I need to tell you," said Sarah.

"From your tone this sounds serious. I hope it's not bad news. And I thought you didn't like to go to the Palmer House," replied Elizabeth.

After an hour's work the ladies headed for brunch. As they arrived at the door of the Palmer House, Sarah stopped momentarily and took a deep breath. She looked up at the grand covering for the entrance and remembered the elegance of the hotel. The doorman held the door open for the ladies to enter.

"Sarah what is the problem? You have me worried," whispered Elizabeth.

"It's alright, Elizabeth. I used to come here all the time with my husband and various friends. I don't want to run into any of them, but I want to enjoy the Sunday brunch here while I tell you about my past life."

It was hard for Sarah herself to understand what made her want to come to this place where she and William and she and Ed had come so often to have this same brunch, but she thought it fitting to tell Elizabeth her story in this setting.

The ladies were seated by one of the enormous windows. After taking in the decorated cove ceiling with the gilded pictures and huge columns from ceiling to the floor, Sarah looked around carefully to determine whether or not any Decaturites or New Yorkers (like Ed) were in the room. Seeing none she relaxed in this familiar atmosphere and began to tell her story.

"You have a right to know who I am and what I have done," said Sarah.

"You mean you aren't Sadie Elwood?"

In a way I am, but that is not my legal name. Sadie is the name my parents gave me but I changed it to a more fashionable Sarah. The Petersen family came from Norway in 1883. My dad farmed in Minnesota and bought lots of land. Being the oldest of three girls and no boys, I held the position of number one farm hand. To reward me for my work in the fields I was allowed to go to school and finally away to business school in St. Paul."

"That's why you are so good at business affairs," chimed in Elizabeth who was beginning to be a little nervous about her good friend and partner's background.

"Well, that helped, but also I met a man, Charles Elwood, who had a successful business and I helped run it. I married him and we had a son named Sam."

"So your real name is Sarah Elwood?" said Elizabeth.

"My life is not that simple."

At that point their food was delivered and Sarah's confession ceased momentarily giving Elizabeth time to digest what she was learning about her partner whom she thought she knew well.

Half way through her food Sarah began to talk again, "My first husband thought it would be fun to have an affair with one of his clients while I did the work at our business. One night I got sick and came home from the office before I was scheduled to, catching him red handed in my bed,"

Sarah took a few bites of her food giving Elizabeth a chance to chime in. "Horrible. But where was your son at the time?"

Sarah glared at her eggs benedict. "I don't even want to say this out loud… My biggest regret in life is that Sam was with his Grandmother Elwood who ended up raising him on the Elwood farm in Iowa. I left Charles and got a very healthy divorce settlement. Waiting until I got settled to bring Sam home, I searched for where home was to be.

This city, Chicago, was where I finally landed and began preparations to bring Sam here. Only in the meantime, I met William Grady, fell in love with him, and got married. Just as I was about to get Sam, William was transferred to Decatur, Illinois. He was obviously going places in his company and needed me to help with entertaining business associates. We were a busy couple."

"And Sam?"

"Yes, finally when he was in high school, he came to Decatur. But, when he was ready for his junior year, both his father and William felt he needed more discipline so he was sent away to military school in Indiana."

"So he had a good upbringing but not with his mother."

"I guess you could say that. After military school, he was accepted into Princeton. Against the advice of both men in his life, he left Princeton at the end of his sophomore year and became a navy pilot. He never went overseas …where he wanted to be… because he contracted the flu…" Sarah's voice broke.

"Oh, Sarah. I'm so sorry, dear friend."

The two women sat silently eating for a bit and then Sarah said, "I was able to be with him when he died in a make-shift navy hospital out East. He is buried in Decatur and I visited his grave almost every day when I lived there."

"I would think Sam's death would have brought you and William closer together."

"No. William was not what I thought him to be. He controlled me, expected me to work literally night and day for him, and physically and mentally abused me. I was a slave."

"How could you have stayed with him as long as you did?"

"Because I fell in love with my soul mate." Elizabeth's eyes widened. After a brief pause Sarah continued, "Yes, I'm a scarlet woman. I had a four year affair with one of William's good friends. His name is Ed and I fell head over heels in love with him."

"I know you well enough to know that you are not a woman to cheat on your husband unless you had good reason."

"I made excuses, but I wanted to divorce William and marry Ed. Ed was a good man and wanted to leave his family, but not with a scandal. However, when things became unbearable with William, I asked Ed to leave his wife and marry me. His only answer was "I'll try to move things along".

"I couldn't accept that answer after our four years together, so I broke it off with him. I lost my soulmate and my soul. Discarding the several years I worked so hard for Prohibition, I started drinking and soon became an alcoholic .Then I made my greatest folly; I started being around another man, another Charles. Love had nothing to do with it. I was just destroyed by my drinking. Destroyed by grief. Destroyed by abuse. I lost the ability to care about anything, especially myself.

"Suspicious of my activities, William hired a private detective to follow me around and soon had enough evidence to file for divorce. The night after the divorce trial William had Charles and I arrested. That was two days before I met you.

"Now you know my name is Sarah Grady and not Sadie Elwood. And you know most of my story. I'm sorry to bring you this scandal. You're such a respectable, kind woman. I hope you don't want to break up our partnership. We're doing really well."

Elizabeth took Sarah's hand, "You're still my partner and I'd still like to call you Sadie. What a story! I'm so sorry you had to go through all that and I now understand why you fear William. I'm sure he didn't feel he had all that coming so he might want to settle the score."

"I probably would have delayed this conversation a little longer except I'm going to take my car to Madison to sell it. I'm sure you would have wondered why I'm selling something that is so dear to me and why I'm not selling it in Chicago. There aren't that many dealers in the U.S. that would have a car like mine on their lot so William could probably track me through the car if he saw fit."

"Actually, Sadie, I have suspected there are things in your life you were not telling me. At the shop the other day when you had gone to the bank a gentleman came in and asked if he could speak to Sarah Grady. He asked about your car and several other things. I told him I'd never seen a car like he was describing and he finally left. I knew he wanted you, but I think I assured him you had nothing to do with our shop."

Sarah breathed a sigh of relief. "It must have been a private detective that William hired to find me. Thanks so much for lying to him."

Elizabeth hugged her friend and they both quietly finished their brunch.

Sarah enjoyed her food thinking *I feel so much better now that Elizabeth knows who I really am and why I fear William.*

CHAPTER 13

★

William Rejoins the World

Decatur, Illinois 1923

William continued living life alone shut up in his house. Besides James, the only contact he had with the outside world was his friend, next-door neighbor, and boss Edward P. Irving. E. P., as he called him, would come over once a week and talk to him.

Mr. Irving was a wise man and didn't try to talk William into leaving the house, but just told him of events that were currently taking place. Gradually William became interested in other things besides himself.

"Faries Manufacturing got word this week that the patent for that ornamental lamp arm you applied for three years ago has been approved. Congratulations," said E. P. Irving.

"You mean that that patent is just now going through?"

"Yeah. It really takes forever."

"Well, what are you doing about it? Have you started making it yet?" William asked.

"We'll get busy on it as soon as you come back to work."

"Well, maybe I could come back to get the process started. I am interested in seeing my invention developed," replied William. "I guess I'll have to go back for a few days."

A tiny bit at a time, E. P. got him out of the house and back to work for a few days a week. William expressed his feelings to his friend. "I need to see Sarah. I can't seem to move beyond this."

On August 17th 1923, William was digesting his breakfast and the newspaper in the breakfast room. Windows were open and he was basking in the fresh morning air. He looked out on the still green grass in the yard separating the Irvings and the Gradys and saw E. P.'s daughter Eleanor walking toward his house. She seemed headed toward his back door. *Why would that be? She would not come calling and certainly not at the back door.*

William heard the knock on the door and James was there to answer it. Their voices floated into the breakfast room and William was aware that something was wrong. *Where was E. P. and didn't Eleanor know that he would not see anyone else.*

James came into the breakfast room and said, "Miss Erving would like to see you for a minute, and I think you should see her."

As William looked at James he knew he needed to say, "Show her in here."

Eleanor's face told the story. Her eyes were red and puffy and her skin was white.

"E. P. is gone?" choked William.

Eleanor nodded her head and said, "Mr. Grady, my mother told me to come over and ask if you would consider being a pall bearer. "

He accepted the honor and decided at that moment that his life would begin anew. Yes, he was done with his grieving and self-pity. William J. Grady would return.

Showing up for work the day after the funeral, he began to implement his invention and let it be known that he was ready to develop other creditable innovations. As Secretary/Treasurer of the company, he found himself in charge because of the death of President Irving.

In that spirit, he went to his travel agent and booked an overseas cruise with several of his friends for February of next year. He thought by that time he would have worked so hard he would be ready for a vacation. The trip would last for two months, and he intended to remember what it was like to have some fun.

William again participated in the activities of the Chamber of Commerce, reminding himself that his goal in life was to become president of Faries Manufacturing. He went back on the board of the Chamber of Commerce…a business must. He returned from a leave of absence to the board of directors for several banks and the Country Club of Decatur. He rejoined any organization he felt would promote his business career.

To the outside world, Mr. Grady seemed normal. At home, however, James was still left with a grieving ex-husband.

"James, get Chad Brown on the phone for me. I need to know what that private detective is doing to earn his money."

James dialed the number until he had the detective on the phone and handed the instrument to William.

"Mr. Brown what have you to tell me about my ex-wife? Have you found her?"

"Sorry to say, Mr. Grady, I have no news yet of Sarah. I thought I might have found her in Bloomington, but that lead turned out to be false. Her car turned up in Wisconsin, but no trace of her. I'm working as hard as I can on your case."

William hesitated for minute deciding whether or not to fire him and then said, "I can't keep you on indefinitely but I'll continue your services for another month. Go find her!"

Without results, William employed the private detective for another month and then fired him. Unbelievably, she was nowhere to be found.

At night visions of punishment chased his sleep. *I need to punish her in some way so I can forget her.*

CHAPTER 14

William Meets Esther

The Majestic 1924

In February, 1924, three years after Sarah's departure from his life, William set sail on the Majestic for a tour of Europe with two of his friends from Decatur, Mr. Bering and Mr. Hitchcock. They were to be gone until the middle of April. William thought this cruise would be the solution for leaving thoughts of Sarah behind him. As he boarded the ship, he had a flashback of another big ocean liner. That one sank taking many lives with it. He remembered the morning he had opened the newspaper and read that the Titanic hit an ice berg and went down. Clear as day he saw Sarah reacting to that tragedy. He shrugged off the picture of Sarah and the sliver of fear that went through him. The Majestic was the largest ocean liner in the world with amenities that echoed the Titanic, and it had a wonderful safety record.

Along with his two friends, he was led to his stateroom. He was satisfied that he would have a grand time.

The steward showed him his room while describing its features. "You'll love the wide window close to your bed; it gives you a spectacular view. Our shower is full size. The chairs are comfortable seating for you and a guest while our beautiful walnut desk provides space for your correspondence. Your room will be kept clean and I will be here to answer any questions you have. Enjoy your trip."

The steward quickly disappeared. William looked around the room at the opulence of his surroundings. The carpet on the floor was lush as were the dark blue upholstered chairs which matched the color of the ocean. The window let in abundant sunlight and the oak woodwork radiated the glowing finish he enjoyed. The Majestic was the first luxury ocean liner he had ever been on.

The Majestic - White Star Line

He expressed his approval to his friends as they met in the swanky bar for a drink. "I think I'll enjoy myself on this trip. The ship is better than I imagined."

"You haven't seen it all yet," said Mr. Bering. "I went down and looked at the swimming pool. It's great for our exercise."

"I can't wait to see the dining room. It's time; let's go and change. You know, we have to be in correct evening attire to eat. I'm showing off my new tux," declared William.

Food was served in a formal dining room complete with chandeliers and white linen tablecloths. As William seated himself at their assigned table, he glanced across the room. *No, it can't be her. Impossible!*

William made a choking, strange, throaty sound and sat down hard on his chair.

"What's the matter?" asked Mr. Hitchcock with concern for his friend.

"That lady with the red dress…across the room… over at the corner table, I thought I knew her," said a discombobulated William. "She looks like someone I used to know, but on second glance, I realize it's not her."

"Ah, yes. She does favor Sarah. My man, you have to get over her. That chapter in your life is gone. Here's to the new one," lectured Mr. Bering as he raised his glass in a toast.

"Yes, to my wife, God rest her soul," William jested to the group, pleased with their boisterous laughter.

Just then two attractive ladies who had been assigned to the table were seated by the wait staff. The three men stood up and William made the introductions giving their names and adding they were from Decatur, Illinois.

The woman seated next to William had an angelic look about her. A tall but slender figure and very well dressed. "My name is Mrs. Esther Bonney and this is Mrs. Martin Rosen. We are from Chicago," declared Mrs. Bonney. .

A lively dinner conversation followed with William being especially interested in Mrs. Bonney because she was a business woman. He learned that she owned a large cosmetic company headquartered in Chicago and the two of them talked marketing all evening. William's friends kept the other woman entertained and at the end of the evening everyone had enjoyed themselves.

The tables in the dining room were assigned for the duration of the trip so the three gentlemen ate all meals with the same two ladies. William soon realized eating was the highlight of his day because he enjoyed talking with Mrs. Bonney.

After dinner the third night at sea, William invited Mrs. Bonney to walk with him on the deck. The scene was gorgeous. Not a cloud in the evening sky. The three-quarter moon shone brightly reflecting on the dark water and stars were poured all over the heavens.

He observed her carefully when they stopped at the rail to look at the black ocean below them. The water was rough and choppy waves banged against the ship. The noise of the whitecaps hitting the metal hull of the boat completed the trancelike scene. Mrs. Bonney appeared... attractive, William thought. Not beautiful like Sarah, but attractive. He wanted to know more about her.

"Tell me about yourself, Mrs. Bonney," said William. "What does your husband do? You haven't mentioned him."

"Please call me Esther. I divorced my husband over ten years ago so I don't know what he does now. My career got in the way of our marriage.

I had a dream to form a cosmetic company using as many natural ingredients in my products as possible, and he struggled to support my vision for our future."

"Without thinking William blurted out, "My wife…I mean my ex-wife, had the same idea, but she was never able to get her products to market. She obviously didn't have your drive."

"Grady… Was her name Sarah? I think I talked with a woman from Decatur who was interested in natural cosmetics and, if I remember correctly, her name was Sarah."

William tightly gripped the rail where he stood and replied, "Yes, my ex-wife's name is…was Sarah."

Esther Bonney could see that she had upset her companion and tactfully suggested that they call it an evening. She remarked that she would see him at breakfast, turned around, and walked away.

William was unable to move. He stood staring at the water that now seemed angry to reflect his mood. He felt nauseous. Maybe he could blame the motion of the ship for feeling sick, but he knew in his heart it was Sarah. The first night at sea, he had thought the woman in the dining room was Sarah. Then tonight he had reacted foolishly when Esther Bonney had mentioned her.

For over three years, he had been unable to discard his thoughts of Sarah. Every day he spent time in reflection. Had he been a bad husband? No. He only expected what every husband did… that his wife be a helpmate and do what he asked of her. In return, he got rebellion and chaos.

He had given her everything and she had humiliated him by cavorting with another man… a waiter turned car salesman. Why did she do that? He had loved her dearly. When would his torture end?

CHAPTER 15

---✦---

Remembering

New York City 1925

Ed Rockafellow watched as the train that was to take him from New York City to Hot Springs, Virginia slowly ground to a halt. He always enjoyed the atmosphere of a depot, but now he carried a bag of mixed emotions. Standing rigidly, Ed watched as the passengers having reached their destination navigated the train's steep steps to the freedom of the platform.

It was time for him to board. **Why** were his legs reluctant to move? He stood riveted to the ground until the conductor called out the familiar "All Aboard." This was it. For the second time in four years, Ed boarded "The Special" to take him to Hot Springs.

The train was not crowded so he could have his pick of seats. *Ok. A window seat in the back of the car. NO! Sarah would not have chosen that one.* He chose a window seat in the middle of the car. *This is where Sarah would have decided to sit.*

The big engine lurched forward and its jerky motion fell into a steady rhythm encouraging Ed to explore his thoughts. He was being sent to Hot Springs to plan a conference for electric workers employed by several large corporations, like in the old days with Western Electric. He relaxed a bit thinking it would be good to get away from Florence even for a few days. The old married couple had had one of their normal spats this morning as Ed was packing for the trip. Swaying back and forth with the train's motion, he considered the events of the morning.

Ed had made his way up the slim attic steps of the New York brownstone he and Florence called home. Upon reaching the top, he entered the neglected, dingy space that was the depository for items that were basically unused but could not be thrown away. Looking around he spotted his trunk over in a corner. The dust had piled up on top of its wooden surface reminding Ed that it had been several years since he had needed a traveling chest.

Reaching the top of the attic stairs, he had taken an extra minute to consider that he was actually getting away for a few days. Away from his new job, away from New York, and away from Florence. He smiled with relief and took a deep, free breath. It should be a wonderful time.

Exhaling forcefully, he blew the thick dust off the trunk revealing several destination stickers displayed on the top. As he ran his fingers over the one that read Hot Springs, Virginia, excitement for his upcoming trip faded into past memories of his days with Sarah at the resort.

He sank to the floor as visions of he and Sarah being together at Hot Springs came flooding back. A vision of her filled the attic in every direction he turned. It had been five years since he had seen her, but she was as vivid in his mind as if he had been with her yesterday.

She disappeared after her divorce from William. *Was she deceased?* He had gone to Hot Springs after her divorce hoping that she would go to their special place as she had indicated in the note she wrote to him on the evening she left Decatur. He waited there for three days but she never showed up. He sensed he would never see her again.

Shaking his head to return to the present, he dragged the trunk to the top of the stairs and then bumped it down the steps.

Florence followed Ed and the trunk he was dragging into their bedroom.

"I'll be leaving this afternoon for Hot Springs," said Ed as he carefully placed a shirt into his trunk. "I need to finish some arrangements for the electric conference in June. I'll just be gone a couple of days."

Florence scoffed, "I can't abide these last minute trips of yours. We've been invited to the Lentz's for dinner tomorrow night and I already accepted. How can I tell them now that we won't attend?"

Staring at the bedroom ceiling to avoid looking at his wife, Ed sighed and continued to pack his clothes. She never ceased to get upset with him no matter what he did. If he stayed home, he would be blamed for not getting out of the house more often. If he went away, she wanted him to be at home. That's the way it was. A trip to Hot Springs was going to provide him with some time alone so he could relax. He looked forward to this business excursion.

Florence tossed herself beside his trunk. "I've been trying to get a dinner invitation to the Lentz's for a long time. I'm sure they'll never ask us again if I cancel so late. Maybe I could go alone and claim a last minute emergency for you."

"It's been years since I've taken a work trip, Florence. I don't wish to be away, but it is vital I do what the company asks so that we can rebuild our former lifestyle. I'm trying to make a good impression on my new company so I can provide for you and the children," said Ed as he finished packing his trunk. "Tell Mrs. Lentz I was called away on business and go by yourself. Take a dozen roses to her and invite them over here when I get back."

"Fine!" said Florence as she huffed out of the bedroom.

After being fired from his prestigious job with Western Electric, he had taken a lesser position with Piedmont Electric. He had lost his edge and was only a good salesman, not a great one anymore.

He had not been a productive employee since Sarah ended their affair. He hated that word "affair". It did not begin to describe the relationship between him and Sarah. She had provided the inspiration to shape him into a dynamic sales manager. Her letters, which came three times a week as a rule, motivated him to be successful. Suddenly, Sarah had written him to stop writing and to never try to contact her again. Ed was stunned even though he knew what the problem was. Sarah got tired of waiting for him to leave his wife and William was getting more and more violent, but the thought of ruining the lives of so many held him back.

Ed had tried for years to invent a way to divorce Florence and marry the one true love of his life. Sarah and he were two of a kind, and Ed believed they were meant to be together. They enjoyed all the same activities. *I remember the first night we met. We were in the garden outside the dining room at Hot Springs Resort and we sat close together on a bench and talked almost until the sun came up.* Both were intrigued by politics, literature, the theater, and golf. Each knew what the other was thinking at any given moment. When they were together, life seemed magical.

Ed had traded stocks for their joint account trying to build up enough profit to sustain him and Sarah for the rest of their lives. He remembered when they had a big disagreement on some coal company stock. Sarah said buy and he said no it was going down. Sarah was right. The stock went up in value considerably. Luckily he had listened to Sarah.

They would need money to be together. He realized if he divorced Florence, he would lose many of his influential friends, probably his job, and thus, a way to earn a living. His wife's powerful family would ostracize him if they felt he had mistreated her.

What irony. When he lost Sarah, he lost his job anyway because he didn't have the drive to be a top salesman without her. Florence was ignorant of his feelings for Sarah so his family was not influenced by his indiscretion. But his loss of Sarah impacted them just the same.

He still had the note she wrote to him on the night she left Decatur two years ago indicating that she still loved him. Despite the fact she was married to one of his good friends, they had been so happy together. *Was it her love for her husband that had caused her to stop seeing me? No, it couldn't have been. Not the way William treated her. I know she loved me. I should have done something different.*

CHAPTER 16

Our Resort

July 1925

Ed left an agitated Florence in the doorway of his house, took a taxi to the railroad station, and now was bound for Hot Springs spending all his time thinking of Sarah. They had stayed in so many places together and every time he visited one of those spots, he thought he saw her. But always it turned out to be an illusion.

Staring out the window of the jerky train, he remembered how she always enjoyed the bumpy ride. It made her feel alive yet peaceful at the same time, she had declared.

As usual the big question loomed in his mind... where was she? He was aware of her disappearance. June Johns, Sarah's best friend and the only one who knew of his connection to Sarah, had written him. June hoped Sarah would have gone to him after her divorce from William. Ed hoped so also, but she didn't come.

He kept in touch with June as he knew she had not given up trying to locate Sarah. He traveled to every place they had been together, trying to find her. He even placed several phone calls to his friend William hoping to be nonchalant and gather information about her whereabouts. However, the reclusive William would not talk to him. After months of no one finding a trace of her, Ed worried that Sarah was no longer of this earth.

The train pulled into the station and the conductor walked through the car calling, "Hot Springs." Ed found it difficult to leave his seat and get off. Once he stepped outside on the platform, he knew his reminiscences of Sarah would intensify.

As he walked down the platform to the station, he could still see the beautiful Sarah glide through the crowd and board the train going west to take her home, while he hopped on the northbound. He even felt the anxiety he experienced when they parted.

It was four in the afternoon when he checked into the Hot Springs Resort and obtained his room key, number 215. *Of course, Sarah's room when we first met. When William left for New York leaving Sarah by herself. Where we first made love. I can't stay there.*

"Excuse me, sir. Would you happen to have another room for me? Perhaps something on the third floor," inquired Ed of the clerk at the desk.

The clerk looked at him quizzically and asked, "Is there something wrong with room 215?"

Ed saw some humor in the situation and briefly considered telling him that he had made love to a good friend's wife in that room nine years ago and then had a four year affair with her. The woman disappeared almost four years ago, but he still loved her and didn't want the memories that room held for him.

But…instead he said, "I just like being up a little higher. It's quieter."

"Of course, here is the key to room 321."

Ed freshened up in room 321 and tried to relax, reminding himself of why he was here. Old memories or not, he intended to eat dinner and then get a good night's sleep. He did have business to attend to.

Ed walked into the familiar dining room and was seated at a table near the dance floor. While waiting for his food, he glanced around the room noting that the starched white linen tablecloths and the floral centerpieces looked the same as when he and Sarah had been here.

His eyes followed a couple around the dance floor where he and Sarah scandalized the crowd by dancing the *Grizzly Bear*. Sarah said William had chastised her for dancing in an inappropriate manner, but he never suspected for a minute that she was being unfaithful to him.

The waiter brought Ed's food and as he started to take a bite, the band began to play his favorite song, his and Sarah's that is. *Smiles* conveyed the message of their love. Ed was entranced. He could see Sarah as if it was 1918 again and she was right beside him. He put his fork back on the plate and pushed the food aside.

When the song ended he snapped back to reality, but he no longer wanted dinner. He wanted Sarah. The memories of her haunted him.

"Sir, is there something wrong with your dinner order?" inquired the waiter.

"Oh, no," said Ed. "Everything is fine. I'm just not hungry."

CHAPTER 17

Surprise

Hot Springs Resort 1925

Ed had tossed and turned in bed all night unable to get Sarah out of his mind. Now he was hungry. His stomach grumbled so loudly that he feared being a source of entertainment to the dining room crowd. He needed to have breakfast, and then accomplish what he had been sent by his company to do.

Walking into the dining room he couldn't believe his eyes. William Grady sat at a table in the center of the room. Ed hoped he was only imagining it. But no, this was real. Sarah's husband, his old friend and colleague, appeared right before him.

William spotted him, so there was no escape. Ed walked reluctantly over to William's table, "What a surprise to see you here. It's been a long time."

William rose from his chair and firmly shook his old friend's hand. "It's great to see you. Been a long time. Join me for breakfast while we catch up."

Ed sat down and tried to wrap his mind around the circumstances that had kept him and William apart. William had become a recluse and he, Ed, had lost his enthusiasm for life. The Grady's divorce and Sarah's subsequent disappearance had wrecked both of their lives.

"A lot has happened to me since I saw you last," said William. "You were very kind to keep inquiring about Sarah's whereabouts." He fell silent and sighed deeply, then continued, "I thought my life was over, but now I have recovered a bit and am back at work... How did you happen to leave Western Electric? You were so good at your job there."

How do I tell him that Sarah was the reason I got fired from Western Electric? Because when your wife left me, I had no reason to keep on going.

Out loud he said, "I actually got let go. I could no longer keep up the hectic pace of the job. My present work at Piedmont Electric keeps me as busy as I want to be."

"How's the family?" inquired William. "Your boy must be grown and darling Gwen a regular lady by this time."

"The children are doing well. Perrine is at Princeton and Gwen is a beautiful eighteen year old." Ed knew he shouldn't broach the subject, but couldn't help himself, "I have to ask. Did you ever hear from Sarah?"

William visibly stiffened. "No. I couldn't find her. All my leads were dead ends. She may be deceased for all I know." William fell silent and then shrugged, "I looked for her mainly out of curiosity anyway."

Ed swallowed hard and changed the subject. "Are you here, like I am, to make arrangements for the Electric Conference this June?"

"Yes. I'm in charge of the presenters. I confess that I also wanted to come to Hot Springs because I so often enjoyed the resort with Sarah. I'm trying to face my ghosts," said William.

Ed smiled, "A catharsis for us all, old boy."

Ed thought breakfast would never end. Each man was absorbed in his thoughts while making light conversation about nothing in particular.

"Let's have dinner together tonight," said William, trying to focus on the social rather than the work he needed to accomplish.

Although Ed dreaded the thought of spending more time with William, he could not think of a good reason why they shouldn't dine together. "I'll meet you here at seven o'clock," Ed agreed and each man went about his business for the day.

Dinner was uncomfortable for both men. Each of them was mired in their inner thoughts and memories of past times at Hot Springs making for very trifling conversation. Ed picked at the steak that had sounded so good when he ordered it and noted that William poured the gin from his flask into his water on too many occasions.

"Were you able to organize the June conference to your liking?" asked William.

"Yes. But now I'm told the company wants me to do the same for a conference in the Midwest in September. So I'll be in your neck of the woods, in Chicago, this summer."

"That's great. While you're there, you must come down to Decatur and spend some time with me. You remember what an easy trip it is on the train. Maybe Florence and the kids could travel with you. Time for us to see each other like before; it's been too long."

"A kind invitation indeed. I know Gwen in particular misses your home in Millikin Place. I'm not sure I'll have time to see you in Decatur, but I'm certain you'll be in Chicago working on the same conference."

Ed couldn't help but smile a little at the invitation remembering how uncomfortable it had been when he and Sarah had been forced to spend time together at the Grady home. They could be much more themselves at the resorts.

Dinner broke up early. Both men took their private thoughts of Sarah and retreated up to their rooms, saying "See you in Chicago."

CHAPTER 18

Sarah Confronts Her Past

Chicago, Illinois Summer 1925

Sarah and Elizabeth were sitting in the garden of their apartment building reading. Looking up from her book a moment, Elizabeth asked, "Don't you think society has gone down the tube? I don't think I'm enjoying Sinclair Lewis. He's making me feel uneasy. So realistic. People are doing evil things today."

"If by evil you are thinking of dancing to Jazz music, wearing dresses like the one I just bought with the short skirt, and women voting , I think we live in a grand time," retorted Sarah.

"You would. You're an activist" said Elizabeth as she returned to her book.

Sarah's mind drifted back as she reflected four or five years ago when she was an activist. *Sometimes I miss that part of my life, but not the husband that came with it.*

Sarah continued, "Don't think about bad things on a beautiful day like today. The only sad part about the day is that it's July 30th which means the summer is more than half gone. Soon it'll be New Year's Eve and we will be ushering in 1926.

"Tomorrow night let's close up the shop a little early and have an elegant dinner at the Palmer House. I feel like celebrating."

Sarah Grady was leading a comfortable life. The millinery shop she started four years ago was showing a hefty profit every month. In fact people were coming to her not only from Chicago but also from some of the eastern cities to buy S & E hats. But more importantly each morning as she unlocked the shop door a tingle went through her. It was love for what she was doing.

Two or three nights a week she went to the theater making sure she was always a first-nighter. Most Saturdays she spent several hours in the Art Institute. Last week she went to the Institute to view a new acquisition *Bathers by a River* by Henri Matisse. Fascinated by a movement in art called "Cubism" she stood for fifteen minutes viewing the work desperately trying to understand the artist's conception, admitting to herself that she preferred realism. *Why couldn't a river look like a river and a woman appear realistically?* Occasionally she allowed herself to remember the time spent with Ed going to art shows. *Ed loved Picasso. We argued all the time about modern art. I guess that's why I'm trying so hard to enjoy it.*

.Every once in a while she would ask herself, *"Are you happy?"* The answer was *"Yes, I am. Sometimes I miss my beautiful house on Millikin Place and the many causes I worked for in Decatur, but not my marriage. I finally am truly happy."*

She worried someday a party of Decatur women might discover the shop, but decided if they came, she could recognize them in time to disappear. Elizabeth or their clerk Nancy could wait on them.

Sarah had a strict rule about men. She would have none of them in her life. After being scorned, led-on, and abused there was nothing more she wanted of "love".

It was not easy for her to keep the men away. She still was a beautiful, unattached, successful business woman. Many men tried to be part of her life, but, while enjoying their attention, she refused to even go to dinner or the theater with them. Elizabeth was a good companion as were other women acquaintances she enjoyed being with.

What do I miss the most from my life with William? …Golf and horseback riding. She needed a man to be able to play golf because none of the golf clubs near Chicago were open to a single woman. She had tried them all. And as far as riding went, she was still grieving over the death of her horse Midnight so no other horse would do. She felt Midnight and her deceased father were the only males in her life that had treated her right.

Not wanting for companionship or money she was happy, but for one thing…she did want to go to Decatur to visit Sam's grave and to see her friend June who by now surely thought she was dead. *"Someday I'll go"*, she thought. *Also I want to make a few changes to my will. When something happens to me I want to be buried with Sam. I'll go to the bank tomorrow and add that direction to my will.*

True to her word, the next day she went to get the will out of her deposit box. The document she had legally drawn up left everything to William. That was fine and would make up for what she had done to him, but really all she wanted was to be buried with Sam.

She considered whether or not to get someone to witness her hand written changes, or to just rely on William or whoever got her will to do what she wanted. Surely anyone would respect her wishes.

She penned her changes and reread the entire piece. Yes, this is what she wanted. Just to be buried with Sam whether it was in Decatur or on Grandma Elwood's cemetery plot in Colo, Iowa. Occasionally she still thought about having Sam's body moved to Grandmother Elwood's grave site, but the details presented too big of an obstacle to overcome.

Putting the will back in the safety deposit box she felt relieved. Things were now right.

WILL OF SARAH O. GRADY

I, SARAH O. GRADY, of the city of DECATUR, county of MACON and State of ILLINOIS, now temporarily residing in the city of CHICAGO, being of sound mind and memory, and under no constraint whatever, do hereby make, declare and publish this to be my Last Will and Testament, in manner following, that is to say:

FIRST: It is my will that all my just debts and funeral expenses be paid by my Executor as soon after my decease as practicable.

SECOND: It is my wish and will that I may be buried with my son, SAMUEL ELWOOD, ~~and that my Trustee make some permanent arrangement of my estate to take perpetual care of our last resting place.~~ *If my Son's remains not already buried at the above family burying ground, my Exec*

THIRD: Subject to the above and foregoing, I give *to that* devise and bequeath all my property, real, personal and mixed, of every kind, nature and character, to WILLIAM G. GRADY, of DECATUR, ILLINOIS, ~~and I trust that he will fully carry out the matter of perpetual care for the last resting place of myself and son,~~ except that he shall pay the sum of $250 00 *Two Hundred + Fifty* DOLLARS to *James D. Gilkee* of *Decatur Ill*. *Same sum to Sadie Nelson of Decatur*

LASTLY: I hereby appoint said WILLIAM G. GRADY to be Executor of this, my last will and testament.

DATED this _____ day of NOVEMBER, A. D., 1921.

Sarah O. Grady (SEAL)

The above and foregoing was duly declared by the said SARAH O. GRADY to be her last will and testament on the day and date above mentioned, and we, in her presence, and at her request, and in the presence of each other, do hereby subscribe the same as attesting witnesses, and we certify that she was of sound mind and memory, and under no constraint at the time she signed and executed said instrument and declared the same to be her will as aforesaid.

Dated this _____ day of November, A. d. 1921

Will of Sarah O. Grady

Fred G. Allen

Pauline Gillette

-ATTESTING WITNESSES-

95

The next evening Sarah and Elizabeth went to the Palmer House as planned and were ushered into the formal dining room.

"Since they remodeled this old hotel, much has changed, but they have kept the elegance and spaciousness of the dining room," said Sarah looking up at the grand chandeliers and trying not to remember the last time she was here with Ed.

"You're right. Who'd have thought that this large three story hotel would be rebuilt and twenty-two more stories would be added," chimed in Elizabeth.

The waiter approached their table. "Hello. My name is Seth and I will have the privilege of serving you this evening," said the formal waiter.

Sarah ordered Lake Trout and Elizabeth said she would try the Lamb with mint sauce. While awaiting their dinner, the ladies relaxed and sipped ginger ale.

"I'm so glad you suggested…," Elizabeth was interrupted by a strange noise coming from Sarah. "Sadie, what's the matter?"

Sarah had pulled her hat down to hide most of her face as she turned bright red. Choking on her ginger ale, she almost whispered, "William and Ed…together…sitting at that table across the room."

Elizabeth spotted two men sitting where Sarah had gestured and all she could think of to say was, "Are you sure?"

Nodding her head "yes", Sarah began to hyperventilate. Elizabeth reached across the table and grabbed Sarah's hand. "Calm down. Take deep breaths."

After a couple of minutes, Sarah seemed herself again. "I'm sorry I lost my footing. Thank you for getting me level again."

Trying to maintain her calm, Sarah fought for control of her thumping heart. "I knew someday I might see one or both of them again, but tonight... and together... is just such a surprise."

At that moment the waiter brought their dinners. Elizabeth began to eat and Sarah nibbled at her food. While deep in thought, Sarah's mood visibly began to change.

"You know, Elizabeth, they would be much more upset to see me than I am to see them. I think I'm going to have some fun. Surely William has forgiven me by now and probably thinks I am dead. I'm going over to their table."

"I'm not sure you are in any shape to confront them. You are still shaky. And you know a lady doesn't walk up to a gentleman's table."

Ignoring Elizabeth, Sarah declared, "I'm okay now. I can pull this off."

"Should I go with you?"

"No. You stay here and watch the entertainment."

Sarah righted her hat, got up from her chair, and walked with grace over to the ex-men in her life. Ed and William were deep in conversation so they didn't notice Sarah until she was standing beside their table. Ed looked up first and stared at Sarah with his mouth wide open. Then William glanced up and recognized his ex-wife. For a moment there was silence as the two men sat motionless and stared at her.

"Good evening, gentlemen. I thought I would come over and say 'hello'."

Ed knocked over his water glass as he struggled to get to his feet. William was slower to react and more deliberate as he also rose from his seat.

"Please, William and Ed, sit down. As I said, I just came over to say hello," said Sarah, totally in control.

William's face was drained of color but his social graces took over as he motioned Sarah to sit down.

"Can't stay. Just wondered what brought you two to Chicago?"

Ed was still visibly shaken and sat quietly staring at Sarah. The waiter interrupted the conversation as he cleaned up the mess from Ed's water glass.

William finally spoke up in a higher tone of voice than usual. Ignoring Sarah's question he blurted out, "I thought you were dead!"

A smiling Sarah said, "I don't think so. I'm very much alive and doing well."

By this time a bewildered Ed had recovered somewhat and questioned, "Do you live in Chicago?

"Yes. I have a lovely apartment and I own and operate the S. & E. Millinery Shop."

William, trying to recuperate from the shock but still the business man, asked, "Where is your shop and is it doing well?"

Sarah was not comfortable giving out too much information. "It's doing very well. I'm still wondering what brought you two to the city."

After a few seconds Ed spoke, "We're planning a big electric conference that will be held here in September."

"Of course. I remember those conferences," said Sarah staring directly at Ed whose face redden. "I trust Florence is well?"

Ed nodded his head yes and both men became silent.

"Well, I'll be going back to my table. Nice to see you. Enjoy your dinners." Sarah turned and walked slowly back to her table.

"How did I do?" Sarah inquired of Elizabeth.

"If you intended to upset them and give both of them a sleepless night, I believe you have been successful. I know you have your back to them, but you would enjoy seeing them sit silently with stunned looks on their faces. Oh… they're getting up to leave now."

The two men had to go by Sarah's table to leave the dining room. Each of them nodded curtly as they passed it.

Sarah gulped the rest of her ginger ale.

"It's been years since I've had to deal with a craving for alcohol, but tonight I could use something stronger."

"I think you did a magnificent job of rattling both of them and you didn't need a drink to accomplish it," said Elizabeth.

"You're right. I got a little revenge on William… and Ed too."

Elizabeth allowed Sarah to sit quietly with her thoughts for a while then suggested they go home."

Sarah was trembling inside but managed to look calm on the exterior. "I guess I spoiled your evening, but it was such a surprise to see them both…together. You know I have no friendly feelings for William. But after everything, I fear I'm still in love with Ed."

Elizabeth trying to lighten the mood said, "Well, I enjoyed the lamb."

CHAPTER 19

It's Just Dinner

Chicago, Illinois August 1925

Sarah sat close to the picture window of her shop staring up at the white fluffy clouds in the sapphire blue sky. The shop had three customers trying on different hats, but she was unaware of them. She was day dreaming while reliving the encounter with William and Ed at the Palmer House several days before.

Seeing William did not rank high on Sarah's "remember this list", but she had enjoyed watching him go pale and struggle to regain his composure when he discovered that his ex-wife was still alive and doing well. But Ed… She had to confess her heart pounded when she stood so close to her former lover.

I must get him out of my mind. He abandoned me when I needed him the most.

"Sadie, Mrs. Gregg needs some help with her choices. Time to get back to work," said Elizabeth patiently.

"Sorry. I was in another world. I'll go help her."

Sarah took care of Mrs. Gregg then walked to the front of the store to replace one of the hats in the display window.

The bell on the front door jingled and Sarah turned to see who was coming in. A tall, slim, handsome man came through the door. *Oh my! It's Ed.*

"How did you find me?" asked Sarah.

"Hello to you too, darling. Could you maybe just say 'hello'? I know you said I should quit writing you, but you didn't say anything about seeing you in person. You know I thought you were dead," said Ed.

Ed handed her a beautifully wrapped box of her favorite Fannie Mae candy. Sarah took the gift and repeated the question, "How did you find me."

"It wasn't very difficult. You mentioned you ran a millinery shop, so I started visiting the hat stores in this area and this is only the fourth one I've been to," said Ed.

Sarah was silent, trying to sort out what her reaction should be. Ed leaned towards her, smiled and said, "Sallie, why don't we have dinner tonight so we could have a chance to talk."

Sarah's breathe caught. *If only he hadn't called me Sallie like he used to, I could have sent him on his way. And even given him back the candy... What would it hurt though to just have dinner with him?*

After a moment of silence Sarah said, "Well, maybe it would be fun to relive some of our past visits together. I'll meet you...and William?"

"I'm staying at the Palmer House. Is that agreeable? William went home right after you stopped by to say hello the other night," said Ed.

"Alright, seven o'clock I'll meet you in the lobby," Sarah said as she walked away. Ed waved and left the store.

"What's wrong with you .You look like you just saw a ghost," said Elizabeth who had been waiting on a customer and hadn't noticed Ed.

"Yes, a ghost of Christmas past. I've just agreed to have dinner with Ed this evening." she sighed. "Undoubtedly it's a big mistake. It's my own fault. I certainly opened a big can of worms the other night,"

"You are a free woman, Sadie. If you want to go out with him, you are legally able to do so."

In spite of telling herself this dinner was not special at all, Sarah spent a good hour picking out the right dress to wear and redid her hair three or four times. The dress she picked leaned toward being on the short side, but it did cover her knees. The soft green of the silk two piece outfit almost made her eyes green. The print on the top satisfied her love of oriental design and the solid colored skirt had a border matching the colorful top. Deciding to wear a hat designed for more formal evenings, she picked out her best fascinator that would allow more of her face to show.

She took a cab to the hotel and as she walked into the lobby several men turned to get a better look at her.

Ed was there waiting and chuckled at her entrance "I see you can still turn heads. You look breathtaking, Sarah. I'm so happy you agreed to have dinner at one of our old places." Sarah couldn't help but beam at him as her cheeks flushed with the memories.

The couple followed the maître'd to the table Ed had reserved near the dance floor. Trying hard to appear unaffected by her former lover, Sarah told herself to breathe slowly and appear pleasant, but it was hard to appear calm when her heart was pounding. She was fascinated and surprised she could feel this new with him after all their former relationships.

Ed didn't fain indifference but went right to what was in his heart. "Sarah, I've missed you so much. I thought you were deceased. I believed all I had of you were my beautiful memories." Ed reached across the table and held her hand in his. "My life hasn't been the same since you walked out of it. My relationship with Florence has gotten worse every year. Without you to cheer me on, I was not able to perform my job very well. In fact, I was fired...'let go' the company said. The truth is I was a mess, my love. I landed a job with Piedmont Electric and thus saved face even though the company is so much smaller and less influential than Western Electric. I..."

Sarah couldn't help being irritated by what Ed was saying. She pulled her hand away from him and interrupted, "You mean you are blaming me for getting fired from your job at Western?"

"Oh, no. I'm only telling you how upset I was when you stopped seeing me."

Sarah's voice got higher and louder, "When I stopped seeing you? Really! If you can remember, we stopped our affair when I told you I needed to get away from William because he was physically threatening me. I told you I wanted to be with you for the rest of my life and you said you couldn't leave Florence at the moment but you would 'work on it'."

"Sarah, I was trying to build up our finances as fast as I could so we could be together. We had to have money to live and Florence controlled most of mine through her inheritance" Ed added, "Please, Sarah, I..."

"We both felt I was in danger staying with William, but you weren't willing to do anything to take me away from him."

"Not true. I was so worried about you and, if you remember, I offered to find you an apartment in New York."

"So I could be your mistress for the rest of my life."

"I had to be practical. My wife's family got me into the circles I ran in. If I left Florence I would have lost my job as well as my influential friends who were my friends because of her connections. I was trying to build up our stock account so it would be enough to take care of us for the rest of our lives. You have my heart and soul."

"No, Ed, You didn't protect me."

Ed hung his head, "You're right I'm ashamed I didn't protect us. I was trying to save everyone as much as I could from my selfishness…from wanting just you every day and I lost it all anyway by not choosing you,"

Sarah's eyes welled with tears as the waiter approached to take their order. Ed ordered dinner for both of them. Gaining her composure Sarah asked, "How are your children? I guess Gwen is a woman now. Eighteen isn't she?"

Ed did a small dissertation on his children. Then as the strains of one of the soft tunes they loved in the past drifted over to their table, Ed extended his hand and said, "Let's have a dance…just for old time's sake."

Inwardly Sarah screamed, *NO. I'll not be able to resist his charm if I dance with him.* Outwardly she took his hand and they glided onto the dance floor.

They were the perfect couple reacting to the music together with the ease of one motion. Neither of them missed a beat. Sarah felt relaxed and safe in Ed's arms, just as though it was six years ago.

The song ended and Sarah turned to go back to their table just as boisterous Jazz music bellowed from the band. Ed grabbed her hand and they were doing their favorite dance, the Grizzly Bear.

They did their moves so well that everyone in the room stopped what they were doing to watch them.

Sarah forgot how mad she was at Ed, how cruel her former husband had been to her, and all the other bad things in her life. She was having a fantastic time. With boundless energy she was living again, all because she was dancing the Grizzly Bear with her soul mate Ed.

They collapsed in the chairs at their table just as their dinner was served. Ed was smiling at Sarah. "See we are still just one when we dance. Can't we carry that over into real life? I bet you haven't had anyone like me to talk politics with you for the last six years."

"And such a pity that is since you would have been throwing the Harding administration up in my face until his death and beyond," quipped Sarah.

"You realize that his wife ran the entire White House?"

"So now we are going into women's rights. You know we have a voice now."

The conversation went on and on until Sarah realized they were the only ones left in the dining room. *Oh, how stupid of you Sarah Grady to fall under Ed's spell again. You know you shouldn't have gone out with him this evening. Nothing's changed in the six years you've been away from him.*

"I must get home. You know I'm a working woman and it's quite late. Aren't you scheduled to leave the city soon?" said Sarah.

"I'm going to come up with an excuse to stay just as long as I can see you. I can't bear to part with you again. But…I understand your reluctance to be with me. May I see you tomorrow evening?" inquired Ed.

"Right now just call me a taxi," said Sarah. We'll see about tomorrow. I have to sort out my feelings."

Sarah spent a sleepless night tossing and turning both her body and her feelings, but got up at her usual time. She went to work and gladly filled Elizabeth in on the details of the previous evening. She needed another evaluation of what was happening between Ed and her. After hearing a bit of Sarah's recanting of her activities with Ed at the hotel, Elizabeth simply said, "From what I gather, he loves you and you love him. Why fight your feelings, Sarah?"

"Ed will never leave his wife, but I don't know if I can take being 'the other woman'." At that moment the phone rang and Sarah answered.

"Hello, Sallie. 'The Lady Who Lied' is playing at the new Uptown Theatre and I was able to get tickets. Please say I can take you to the theater tonight."

This was the new theatre that Sarah wanted to see. She had missed opening night, but now she could go with Ed. Knowing full well what she was doing, she said, "Pick me up at my apartment about 6:30."

"Splendid," said Ed.

Sarah rationalized that she wanted to see the new theater more than Ed. But even she did not believe it.

"Elizabeth, can you watch the store for an hour or so. I need to go out."

"Sure. Where are you going?" asked Elizabeth.

"I feel the need to go see Madame Lily. She does seem to know what's going on in my life. I need to ask her a question."

Elizabeth chided her, "I thought you didn't believe in astrology."

"Right now I think the stars know better than I do if I'm doing the right thing by going out with Ed. I won't be long."

Madame Lily ushered Sarah into her inner room and immediately began to tell her what she wanted to know. Gazing into the crystal ball on the table she pronounced, "The stars are showing me that you will be very happy with a married gentleman."

Sarah smiled and asked "Do you see anything else?"

"Yes. Your shop will prosper. Customers will come from all over the country."

Sarah felt happy with her reading and got up to leave. But Madame put out her hand and said, "Wait. Listen to the stars."

Sarah sat back down into her chair expecting more good news. Madame Lily was looking deep into her crystal ball, then turned to her cards and began to lay them out on the table. Sarah began to fidget. It was taking so long. After looking at the cards Madam Lily slowly made her prediction. "Under no circumstances should you to return to your former home." Madame Lily stopped her forecasting and held Sarah's face in her hands repeating the seriousness of her last prediction. "Never return to your former home. I see death there for you," pronounced the clairvoyant.

Sarah felt a cold chill go through her. Sobered by the last declaration from the Madame, she ended the session and left.

I don't really believe in the stars. Perhaps Madame Lily has made up something to keep me coming to see her... That has to be the problem. At least she thinks I should see Ed.

CHAPTER 20

Fire!

Chicago, Illinois September 1925

The Uptown Theatre did not disappoint either Sarah or Ed. The five story lobby with much gilt and glamor was breath-taking. The exceptional architecture did not quit as they were ushered to their plush velvet seats. Both Ed and Sarah found the play intriguing and well-produced, making their theatre experience perfect.

With Madame Lily's blessing, Sarah had accepted Ed's invitation and had decided to enjoy the evening and not worry about her relationship with Ed. With robust appetites they consumed a lovely dinner in a small Greek restaurant to end the evening. Then Ed hailed a taxi so he could take Sarah home.

The perfect outing turned sour about a block from Sarah's apartment when they found a police wagon blocking the street. It was late, about eleven-thirty, and a big crowd of people was gathered on the sidewalks, some in their night clothes.

"Officer, what's the problem? I'm trying to escort this lady to her apartment down the street," inquired Ed.

"Sorry, sir. Is her home in the hotel apartments on Kenmore?" asked the officer.

Sarah piped up, "Yes. What's the matter?"

About that time she looked up and saw a big cloud of black smoke coming from the area where her apartment was.

"It's fire in my building," choked Sarah. "Is it bad?"

The officer said, "I'm sorry, Miss, I don't have much information. I understand everyone got out of the building unharmed. As to the fire itself, I don't know. What I can suggest to you is find somewhere to stay tonight because I'm sure you won't be able to go to your home at least not until morning and maybe not then."

"I need to find Elizabeth. She must be scared to death. I've got to get closer to see how bad it is."

"Sorry, Miss. I can't let you through," said the policeman.

Ed could see that Sarah was having a hard time keeping control of herself. "Sarah, there is nothing you can do." Their taxi was still there as Ed hadn't paid his fare yet. Grabbing Sarah's arm Ed said, "Come on. We're getting out of here."

As she protested, Sarah allowed herself to be tucked into the back seat of the taxi and Ed told the driver to take them to the Palmer House.

When the taxi pulled away Sarah gave control to Ed and uncharacteristically started sobbing. "Oh, Ed! This is the third time I've lost everything. I'm not as strong as I pretend to be. I'm alone...I can't do this again."

"My Sallie, I'm here. You're not alone and all you could lose are 'things' that can be replaced...and you don't know if the fire will destroy your apartment. You stay with me tonight and tomorrow I'll help you get settled again."

Sarah allowed herself to be led up to Ed's room at the hotel. *This will end in disaster for me.* But his arms around her as she wept were such comfort. To finally have the one who could hold her pain for her was too relieving and attractive to decline.

When they got to his suite, Ed pulled a flask out of his suitcase. "I'm still true to our old pledge to not drink when we are out in public, but I do keep some brandy for emergencies like this. He fixed her a drink and they collapsed into the easy chairs.

The brandy started to have an effect and Sarah began to do what she always did in a tough situation …talk. "I'm glad you were here for me tonight. I don't know what I would have done without you. I'm awfully worried about Elizabeth." Sarah droned on and on expressing every anxiety of her head and heart until no words were left.

Seeing how upset she was Ed fixed her another drink which she downed rather quickly. He turned his back on her to get a drink for himself and, when he sat down in his chair, Sarah's diatribe stopped. She was sound asleep. The brandy had worked.

Getting a blanket from the closet, he tucked it around her and removed her hat. He whispered to her, "My Sallie, I've missed you so much. For six years I haven't felt alive." Then he lay down on the nearby bed feeling that Sarah was set for the rest of the night.

Sarah awoke to Ed offering her a steaming cup of coffee. "Is it morning? Have I been asleep long?"

"Yes and yes," answered Ed.

"How could I sleep when my apartment may be gone and Elizabeth …who knows"?

"I think the brandy helped you get a fair night's sleep. I've ordered breakfast up to our room. It should be here any minute. After we eat we'll go and see what damage has been done to your apartment," said Ed calmly.

Sarah got up from the chair and looked in the mirror. Even with all her anxiety about the fire she was concerned that she didn't look her best.

The bell boy knocked on the door with their breakfast.

"I couldn't eat a bite" said Sarah.

"Just sit down and drink your coffee while I have something and maybe you can eat a little bit."

Sarah started taking 'just a bite 'and soon had consumed her entire breakfast. Satisfied she was in good shape, Ed said, "Let's go check out your building."

CHAPTER 21

Just Smoke

Chicago, Illinois September 1925

Sarah's apartment was in the front part of the building. As the taxi pulled up to the main entrance, she noted that nothing seemed different except there was a police car parked at the curb and a fire truck sitting behind it.

"Oh, Ed. Look! From the street it appears like my home is still intact. Please hold my hand while we go inside."

A policeman hopped out of his car as the two of them began walking towards the front door. "Do you have a reason to go inside?" he asked.

Sarah sounded a bit quarrelsome as she answered him. "Until the fire last night I lived here. I need to see if my place is alright."

"Your name please," said the policeman pulling out a tablet from his pocket.

"Sarah Grady."

"Okay, Mrs. Grady. I see you live in 2B. It's safe for you to go inside."

Ed paid the taxi and hand in hand they walked inside the building. Sarah dropped Ed's hand and ran up the stairs that led to her apartment. She stopped and took a deep breath as she looked at her front door that had been kicked in and was standing wide open.

Walking deliberately through the whole place, she finally said, "Ed, I can't see anything that is even out of order. It's just that horrible smell...the smoke. It almost chokes me."

At that moment Elizabeth walked through the open door. Running towards her friend she cried, "Sadie! I've been so worried about you. Are you alright?"

The two friends hugged for a full minute until Sarah noticed a man standing in the doorway. He nodded to her and Sarah couldn't help but smile. Elizabeth's friend was none other than Richard Parker, her soon-to-be ex-husband whom Sarah had put to shame several weeks ago when he flirted with her in the apartment lobby.

He came inside and stood beside Elizabeth putting his arm around her in a protective gesture. Sarah wondered about the situation but found no words.

"Your things look like they are in good shape except for the smell of smoke. Mine too. How lucky we are. Did you see that the whole back third of the building was destroyed?" asked Elizabeth.

Sarah replied, "Oh, goodness gracious! No, I haven't seen anything of the actual fire. Where did you go last night? I was worried about you."

"Thankfully she had sense enough to call me and I came and picked her up," said Richard as he looked down at Elizabeth with an adoring smile. "Even though she was upset we had a lovely evening."

Sarah raised an eyebrow to Elizabeth who looked down momentarily. Pulling Sarah aside Elizabeth explained, "Sadie, Richard has changed his attitude about many things and I believe we have a chance to patch up our marriage. Our divorce has not become final yet," explained Elizabeth.

Sarah was not convinced that Richard had changed and would be a good husband for Elizabeth, but realized, considering her own circumstances, she should be supportive of her friend.

"Broken bones heal stronger," said Sarah. Elizabeth squeezed Sarah's hand in gratitude.

"Where did you go last night?" asked Elizabeth.

Ed replied for Sarah, "I took her to my hotel when the police told us she couldn't get in here."

There was a knock on the open door and the apartment manager appeared.

"Good. Both you and Elizabeth are here," said the manager. "We'll be starting our cleaning tomorrow morning. I promise you'll never know the fire happened when we get through. Our security will be in place until your door is fixed. I would say you could move back in two or three days."

The manager walked out around the broken door and Elizabeth and Richard started to leave.

"You can stay with us if you would like while the apartments are being cleaned and repaired," said Elizabeth.

Sarah was still gazing around the room for things out of place. "Sorry. I wasn't paying attention. What did you say?"

"No need to worry about Sarah. I'll get her a room at the Palmer House and take good care of her, Elizabeth," said Ed.

Sarah sank down into her couch, "This really smells like smoke… I'll be alright," she said to her friend.

Elizabeth looked at Ed who shook his head in approval. "She'll be okay."

Elizabeth took Richard's arm again. As they walked out the door she turned and winked at Sarah. "I am going home now with my husband."

Sarah looked at Ed who sat down on the couch beside her. "Thank you for looking after me."

"I wish for nothing else."

"We have to get out of here. The smoke smell is horrible," choked Sarah.

CHAPTER 22

Life Moves On

Decatur, Illinois September 1925

William returned to Decatur the day after he and Ed had encountered Sarah in Chicago. The shock of seeing her kept him awake for several nights as he tried to sort out his feelings. He recognized the upset as normal because he believed her to be dead, but he found it hard to accept the joy he felt upon seeing her alive. He hated her. Despised her. Loathed her. Death was not enough punishment for what she had done. But she was alive and flourishing and he was still suffering. *How can I be happy she is alive?*

No one in Decatur had seen or heard from her and most assumed she was deceased. Some people thought she had probably committed suicide after her indiscretions were made public. William briefly wondered if he should call June and tell her that Sarah was alive. *No... Sarah was dead to Decatur, even to her best friend.*

William's upset led him to make a decision to lead a happy life himself. He needed a new partner. That is what he missed about Sarah, having someone to help him attain his business goals. He now owned a small coal company, but his main object still was to become President of Fairies Manufacturing. In order to become the top man he needed more money to buy a bigger share of the company. He was in good shape financially but a great deal more cash would be necessary to buy the position of President.

Someone would have to take Sarah's place and he determined he knew just the person, Esther Bonney, the woman he met on the ship coming home from his trip to Europe. He and Esther had seen each other several times in the last year when he went to Chicago. She was not beautiful or stunning like Sarah, but carried herself in a fairly attractive manner and was a pleasant conversationalist.

William tried to look at her logically. She was a business woman, she owned and operated a very successful cosmetic company, and she was exceptionally wealthy. Also, she owned valuable farm land in central Illinois. Her negatives were people did not take to her as they did to Sarah, and Esther would not always be around to entertain his business associates as she had to spend much time in Chicago with her own business.

As William pondered his future, he made plans to return to Chicago to see Esther. Each time he visited her, he couldn't help thinking of Sarah being close by and wondering if he should go see her. Although he still wanted revenge on his former wife, he decided to concentrate on his new life.

In December he went to Chicago to see Esther. "Let's have dinner at the Palmer House tonight. I'll pick you up around 7:00." *Why did he always pick the Palmer House where he and Sarah always went…especially on this occasion?*

It was a cold winter night making the two of them huddle together in the taxi. Esther couldn't put her finger on it, but she sensed something different about the dinner they were to enjoy in a few minutes. Hardly had they been settled at their dinner table when he said "Will you marry me, Esther?"

"I know this is not a young romantic relationship, but I am very fond of you. I believe that marriage would be good for both of us. We enjoy each other's company and as a couple we could enhance both of our businesses."

Esther had hoped for this proposal but took a moment before she answered. "That's not much of a proposal but I have confidence in your premise and... I'm afraid I'm in love with you. If you can be true to me and be a reliable companion, then I accept your proposal," said Esther understanding what she was agreeing to.

They planned a small ceremony for the spring of 1926.

———————————

Trying not to make too big a deal out of his second marriage, William entertained his male friends at a dinner to announce his engagement less than a week before he was to be married near Chicago.

On May 26, 1926 William and Esther were married in La Grange, Indiana with only a few relatives and close friends attending. Leaving on an automobile trip to the east in William's new car, they planned to be gone about two weeks and then return to make William's #3 Millikin Place their home. William struggled with that decision because every nook and cranny of his home reminded him of Sarah. *I will bury them in new memories.*

After his marriage he spent his time making the dream of becoming President of Faries Manufacturing a reality. Since marrying Esther his financial position had improved to the point that it was only a matter of time before he could claim his reward. Their rather platonic relationship seemed to be working out just fine and William was too busy to spend time dwelling on the ghosts of Sarah, real or imagined.

CHAPTER 23

Forgiveness

Chicago, Illinois Fall 1925

Sarah allowed Ed to remove her from the smoke filled apartment she called home and take her to his hotel where he registered her for a room close to his.

As they were going up on the elevator Sarah began to take in the reality of the situation. "I don't have anything with me. No fresh clothes, no night clothes, no anything,"

"Make a list of what you need and I will secure you any essentials… and non-essentials," he added with a smile. "It will be alright Sallie."

Ed stopped at room 235 and pointed out to Sarah that he was in room 236 right across the hall. "I explained to the front desk as we checked in that you were here because of a fire which is why you have no luggage. The hotel personnel won't disturb you."

Ed unlocked her door and gave her the key. "Please go lie down and rest. I'll come for you about 6:30 and we'll have dinner here."

"I can't go to dinner. I have no appropriate attire yet."

"Forgive me. We'll call for room service."

Sarah was about to protest but was just too depleted. The events of the last couple of days caught up with her. "Fine," she resigned as she closed the door to her newly acquired hotel room. She glanced around the room and uncharacteristically had no thoughts about the décor. The bed looked inviting so she threw herself down on the mattress and fell asleep.

A light knock on her door woke her up. She glanced out of her window and saw that it was barely light outside.

"Who is it?" Sarah asked.

"The man seeing to it that you get some food," replied Ed from the hallway. "I've already ordered room service."

Sarah opened the door letting Ed inside. Sitting back on the edge of the bed she began to gather her thoughts. There was no longer any reason for her to be upset. The fire had not permanently damaged her apartment. She could go back home in a day or two. Elizabeth was handling the hat shop and here she was sitting with him, Ed. The focus of her every thought for four years. Her secret respite from the awfulness of the world. From the loss of Sam. From the boredom of her social circle. Her intellectual match. Her lover.

Memories flooded her mind and body and her fingertips could almost feel the thousands of sheets of prose passed between them through the years. And hearing every utterance of admiration, Sarah Grady so steadfastly future-focused was overwhelmed with gratitude for Ed's existence in the current moment before her very eyes. Not locked away in a letter. Not trapped in a shame filled past. She was free of William and she, at last, could do what she wanted.

Losing all modesty Sarah flung herself across the room into Ed's lap.

"I thank God you are here Ed, I do miss you. I miss you more than I care to admit."

Ed relaxed into her embrace, but felt he had to ask, "Why didn't you meet me, Sarah? I know you were angry, but you wrote me and said you were going to our special place…and when you didn't show I thought that bastard might have killed you or driven you to suicide. Why? Why did you terrify me so? Don't you know life is all for nothing without you?

Ed hugged Sarah tightly and continued, "I was going as fast as I could toward getting you settled away from William. I love you more than you'll ever know."

Sarah's eyes became misty and she spoke softly, "When I felt you had abandoned me, I was so heartbroken that I turned to a wild life. The moral life we tried to lead together was gone and I replaced it with men and alcohol. My marriage was over. William got more and more abusive and you were gone. I no longer cared about anything. I'm sure you can never forgive me. I wrote you that awful day of my arrest because part of me wanted to recoup our relationship. And then I realized I had ruined everything we had. Who would want anyone who had made the front page of the newspaper after being arrested basically for adultery?"

"But you are wrong, Sallie. I was the one at fault and I certainly don't blame you for your actions. I blame myself for not being able to care for you. My fault for taking so long to make you mine."

After a long kiss, Ed held her face in his hands and looked into her eyes saying, "None of that matters now. I don't care about your indiscretions. I don't care that you didn't show up. You're alive. I'm alive. That's enough for now."

After contemplating for a moment, Ed continued, "Let's forget the past five years and look to the future. I called Florence and told her there was some trouble here and it would be three more days before I could get home. I am still married but at least you are free now."

Sarah swallowed hard as she recognized the problem of Florence still stood between them. *I can do this. I can be the mistress because I love him so. I haven't been this happy since I was with him five years ago.* Out loud she said, "We have three whole days to be together. Let's make the most of them."

Their room service arrived and Sarah consumed the whole meal which was the most sumptuous that she had ever eaten. Ed had remembered all of her favorites.

"In the morning we are going golfing. I know…you don't have any clothes. There will be a golf outfit arriving first thing in the morning. I've taken care of that."

"But it may not fit me," protested Sarah.

"It'll be perfect. I certainly know your size which hasn't changed in the last five years. " Ed said with a devilish wink.

They embraced and just like old times, they made passionate love and then talked throughout the night. Literature was the first topic. Both had read many books in the last few years that they hadn't had a chance to discuss.

"I'll bet you know what my favorite book has been for the last several years," said Ed with a twinkle in his eyes.

Sarah responded quickly, "Of course I do. It has to be *The Great Gatsby*. There is so much in that story that we can relate to. So many similarities to our lives. I've read and reread the book many times. Sometimes I loved it and sometimes I hated it. I don't know which character I identify with the most. Nick crazed in an asylum? Gatsby forever after Daisy? Jordan golfing and watching it all? Oh, you're the pro golfer of our own Gatsby. As long as Florence doesn't run you down and I don't end up face down in the pool, I'll be thrilled."

They both laughed.

"Let's make our own ending," said a cheerful Sarah, squeezing her arms tightly around him.

Ed's tone of voice suddenly became serious, "I know what you mean by loving and hating it, Sarah. How could I not identify with Gatsby after my childhood and our relationship? I know what it is to feel like an imposter all my life and love a woman married to another. Decatur, Illinois has long been my green light."

Sarah's breath caught. How often she had felt the same longing. How she had denied herself even the privilege of thinking of feeling that longing. She had filled her days with work and tried to forget. But hearing his voice and feeling the comfort of his arms around her…she could forget no more. Ed was with her and nothing else mattered.

The topic changed to politics and the couple found much to disagree about. As of old, the so called 'independent' Ed chastised the Republican, Mid-Western Sarah for believing that Warren Harding was a good President.

"His term was full of scandal and besides his wife ran the office. When Florence Harding couldn't keep the scandals at bay she killed her husband," said Ed.

Sarah retorted, "She did not kill her husband. That's just a horrible rumor. She ran the show and did a great job. Welcome to the ingenuity of women, America."

On and on the dialogue went with both parties enjoying it immensely. Finally in the wee hours of the morning they both fell into a blissful sleep in each other's arms.

The next morning Sarah's golf outfit arrived and she couldn't believe how well it fit her. Ed went to his room to get into his proper clothes. By nine o'clock they were off in a rental car.

"Where are we going?" asked Sarah. "You know I haven't played golf in years. Not since my leaving Decatur. I hope you haven't gone to any trouble to set this up."

"Nothing is too good for my Sallie. I bet you can still come close to beating me. We'll soon find out."

As Ed spoke he turned the car into a long driveway. Large elm trees lined the way to an 80 foot high clock tower.

As the tower came into view Sarah gasped, "Ed, this is Olympia Fields. Oh, look at the clock tower. Are you a member here? I hear they have four eighteen-hole courses here."

"Yes, I do belong thanks to my company. I have need of entertaining clients when I come to Chicago. I 'm glad you can still get excited over a golf course," said Ed.

"Not just a golf course…Olympia Fields. Do you know this is the largest course in the world?"

After the club manager found the appropriate clubs for Sarah, they stepped up to tee off of the first hole. *I'm nervous.* It had been so long since she had held a club in her hands that she didn't know what to expect. After several practice swings, sensing her reluctance Ed said, "Go ahead and hit the ball, Sarah. Your shot will be good." Swinging with all her might, she was delighted to see her shot go straight and further than could have been expected. Sarah was relaxed and delighted to be playing golf again, especially at such a prestigious club. She was unable to beat Ed but played a respectable game.

The three days they had together were the happiest, most memorable Sarah had ever experienced. They rode horses, went to the theater twice, and even made it to the Art Institute. At night she laid in Ed's arms where she felt safe and loved. *I don't have to consult Madame Lily to know that Ed is my one and only true love no matter his marital status.*

The plan was for Ed to return to Chicago in a month. Sarah went back to her apartment where she found the smoke smell gone, even from her clothes.

CHAPTER 24

Happiness

Chicago, Illinois 1926-1928

The years 1926 through 1928 brought Sarah the happiest memories she had ever had. William became a distant recollection. The only time she thought of him was when she saw a small article in the Chicago Tribune saying that he had been made President of Faries Manufacturing. In spite of all that had happened, she realized she was happy for him and wondered if it would now be safe for her to go back to Decatur to visit her dear friend June and Sam's grave. As she pondered a trip to Decatur, Madame Lily's prediction of death, if she returned, popped back into her head. Sarah did not believe in fortune telling but somehow could not forget what the stars had foretold. Also for some reason, which seemed weird to her since she believed the predictions were mumbo jumbo, she felt the need to check with the Madame when she had a problem. The clairvoyant had foretold Sarah's life pretty well so far.

I'll put off my visit to Decatur for a while longer, but I do want to go back especially to visit Sam's grave.

As the stars predicted, the S & E Millinery shop continued to grow. In fact it became so big that Elizabeth decided to back out of their partnership.

"Sadie, I'm so sorry but I can't keep up with the pace of our successful business. You know I'm still working hard at my marriage and Richard agrees that I should quit. I can make a few hats for you but I need to stop the daily grind," said Elizabeth.

"I'm sorry you want to leave our shop, but I understand. The shop was my idea to begin with and you only came aboard because you had an unsettled marriage. So glad your husband is behaving himself and you two are happy. I've missed you being across the hall from me, but now, at least once in a while, I have Ed to brighten my life."

Not feeling the need of an attorney, they sat down at a desk and dissolved the partnership leaving Sarah as the single owner of S & E Millinery. Although she hated to lose her partner, being an aggressive business woman, she was happy at the prospect of being able to expand the shop. The building next door was available and Sarah knew exactly what she could do with it. Elizabeth had been holding the business back somewhat so now it was time to charge ahead. Sarah alone would now have to gather most of the store's inventory. This circumstance delighted her because that meant many trips to New York to buy hats… and see Ed.

At quitting time, after her conversation with Elizabeth, Sarah went outside and locked the door to the shop, still engrossed in her thinking about Elizabeth leaving the partnership. They were still the best of friends so Sarah was not worried about their relationship. As she turned onto the sidewalk from the shop door, she bumped into a little girl.

Sarah surmised the little girl was about five years old. She had golden hair, deep blue eyes, and was wearing a ragged sweater. The little girl looked up at her. Sarah had never seen such a sad look on the face of a child.

"Oh, honey, I am sorry. I wasn't looking where I was going. Did I hurt you?" said Sarah.

The little girl shook her head "no", but did not move.

"Where are you going?" No answer.

"Where are your parents?" No answer.

"What is your name?"

The little girl looked up at Sarah again with her sad, sweet face. "My name is Ruby."

"Hi, Ruby. My name is Sarah. Could you tell me where you are going?"

The little girl hesitated but then spoke in a soft voice, "I'm going to find my Mommy."

Suspecting something was wrong Sarah asked the little girl if she wanted to come into the shop for a bit.

Another shake of the head this time in the affirmative. Sarah opened the shop again and the two went inside and sat down. After a half an hour of trying to gain information, Ruby had given only meager details. Sarah believed Ruby was trying to find her parents, but had no idea where to look. There was a Miss Graham whom she was staying with…somewhere.

"We have to find Miss Graham. She will be worried about you," said a discouraged Sarah. She hated to call the police because she thought it would scare Ruby. Suddenly a picture of an orphanage about a half mile down Kenwood popped into her mind. Not remembering the name of the institution so she could call on the phone, Sarah suggested she and Ruby walk there. *It was worth a try.*

All the way to the orphanage Ruby was silent and Sarah tried to chatter cheerily. Upon arrival Sarah asked to see a Miss Graham.

"Oh, you found Ruby," the pleasant matron at the door exclaimed. "We have been so worried. Come in you two."

All three went into a cheery reception room and Miss Graham and Sarah exchanged names as they sat down.

"Ruby, where have you been? We have been looking all over for you," said Miss Graham. "Why don't you go in the kitchen and ask cook for a cookie."

"Can't I stay with Sarah? She might be able to help me find my mommy."

"Not now. Go on and see cook."

Ruby turned and slowly left the room with a dejected look on her face.

When she was gone Sarah turned to Miss Graham for an explanation.

"Thank you so much for bringing her back. We thought she was in the library and just a few minutes ago realized she was gone."

Sarah asked for more details, "Ruby said she was looking for her mother. Where are her parents?"

"Ruby doesn't understand that her parents are deceased. They were both killed in an automobile accident. We have tried to get her to understand, but haven't been successful. There is no other family so Ruby was assigned here. She is such a sweet little girl, I wish there was more we could do. Some family could adopt her, but so far Ruby has been resistant to a new home."

"What a sad story," said Sarah as she immediately contemplated adopting a child. *I don't have the time for a child, but I have to do something.*

On impulse Sarah asked, "Could I take Ruby home with me for just a few days? Maybe I could get through to her about her parents."

"She seems taken with you so I'm sure she would like that. I'll have to put your name up for approval, but that shouldn't take long," said Miss Graham.

Ruby came back into the room with an uneaten cookie in her hands.

Miss Graham said, "Honey, would you like to spend a few days with Sarah?"

The words were hardly out of Miss Graham's mouth when Ruby started jumping up and down. Sarah had already caught her heart. "Yes, yes. Can I go now?"

"Not now but soon I hope. For now, tell Sarah thank you for bringing you home. Sarah, I'll be in touch with you as soon as I can."

Sarah went home wondering what she could do for Ruby. She had no business taking on a child, but longed to be able to assist her. She missed her time in Decatur when she spent a great deal of her day working with orphans and others that needed help. Now all she had time for was her shop and Ed. But somehow she would help Ruby.

The next morning Miss Graham called to tell Sarah that she had been cleared to take Ruby to her home for a visit.

Knowing how anxious Ruby would be, Sarah said, "I'll pick her up at four- thirty this afternoon and hope she can stay for several days."

The two of them spent three days together. Sarah took Ruby to the shop with her. Ruby loved the atmosphere and the hats. Sarah found a hat that was just right for a little girl and took much time trying to explain why she would not find her parents in Chicago.

Although tempted to adopt, Sarah had to be realistic. With the total weight of the shop on her now that Elizabeth was no longer part of it, she did not have the schedule to allow being with Ruby all the time. What she did was sign Ruby up for weekends with her and sent money to the orphanage to help the whole organization.

Ruby allowed Sarah to make up a little for what she had missed with her own child. Sarah felt happy to be of help to others. This is what she missed most of all about her former life.

CHAPTER 25

Jiggers!

Chicago, Illinois 1928

Every month the S & E Millinery grew both in reputation and customers. Sarah even had to dodge some of her old friends from Decatur. She thought it best not to try to renew old relationships. When Decaturites came into the store, Sarah quickly disappeared for a while. Most of them still thought she was deceased and she saw no reason to change that. She was sure William had not mentioned to his friends that he had seen her in Chicago.

One day, however, she had an unsettling experience. It was late afternoon. Glancing around her shop Sarah noted the store was still very busy for this time of the day. She had intended to work in her office catching up on paying bills, but the store had been so busy all day that she had to spend her efforts on the floor. Just as she headed for the office another customer came through the door. Seeing that all the sales girls were busy, she realized this customer was hers.

She approached the woman and said, "Good afternoon. Welcome to S & E Hats. How can I help you today?"

The woman answered Sarah by saying she was just looking for an every-day hat to wear for afternoon meetings. As she sat in front of the mirror and began trying on hats, Sarah was a bit puzzled. This woman looked familiar to her. Mentally, Sarah went through her repertoire of persons trying to place her. *Previous customer? No. From New York? No. Met her with Ed at a resort? No.*

Suddenly it came to her. *This is the woman who ran a large cosmetic company that I met in Chicago when I was married to William. Oh my gosh! She is, or was, Esther Bonney who is now the new Mrs. William Grady.*

Making a pretext of bringing Esther another hat Sarah slipped into her office and tried to compose herself. She was sweating and hyperventilating. *Get hold of yourself, Sarah. She is showing no sign of recognizing you. William would not have told her I was alive. I still feel safer if no one knows I'm alive but Ed.*

Taking four deep breaths to pull herself together, Sarah took Esther another hat and said, "I'm going to send Nancy to help you make a decision."

Esther looked up directly at Sarah as though there was some sort of recognition. Shaking her head just slightly then pausing, she turned back to the mirror. "Fine. I think I've almost made up my mind."

Sarah hurried to Nancy who was helping someone else and whispered to her. "Please take care of that woman in back. She is from Decatur and I don't want her to know who I am. I'll take your customer." Nancy did as requested and soon the new Mrs. William Grady walked out the door with a lovely new hat.

Sarah went home, made a hot cup of tea, and sat down in her favorite chair to ponder why she was so upset. She had left Decatur in disgrace and didn't want to visit that part of her life again. She decided she was correct in being secretive about her present life. After all she was happy, she was with Ed, and she had a very successful shop with the present Mrs. William Grady in her list of customers.

Ed managed to visit Chicago at least every other month and Sarah was able to go to New York frequently to purchase hats for her shop. Life was as Sarah had imagined it should be. They wrote at least two letters a week to each other. Occasionally they would spend a few days together at a resort such as French Lick or Greenbrier registered as Mr. and Mrs. Edward Rockafellow.

Registration at the Greenbrier almost disclosed their secret life when Florence went to the resort with one of her friends for a week-end trip. The clerk at the front desk greeted her with a, "So nice to see you so soon again Mrs. Rockafellow. I see we have given you the same room that you had last week."

"So soon… same room? I haven't been here for five years," replied Florence.

"But you just signed in last week," said the clerk.

Quickly realizing there was a problem that probably shouldn't be addressed he stammered, "I'm so sorry. I have you mixed up with someone else. Forgive me. It's nice to see you."

Confused, Florence put the incident down to a poor employee. "In a place like this they should be more careful who they hire to take care of the guests," said Florence to her friend.

Several times Ed and Sarah were almost caught together in New York. Sarah was in the big city for several days on a buying trip for her store and Ed had made dinner reservations for them at the Biltmore where

Sarah was staying. He had been held up with business so Sarah was sitting alone in the dining room waiting for him. Of all the places to eat in New York, Florence had chosen the Biltmore on this evening to have dinner with a friend. As the real Mrs. Rockafellow was being escorted to her table she saw Sarah seating alone.

People do change a bit in nine years so at first Florence was not sure it was Sarah. She was seated close to Sarah's table and kept staring at her. Finally she rose from her seat and went to encounter her.

"Excuse me," said Florence. As soon as Sarah looked up from her table Florence cried out, "It is you! Sarah Grady."

Sarah didn't know how to react. Florence had always considered Sarah as one of her best friends and even sought martial advice from her. Now sitting here waiting for Florence's husband to come to dinner and spend the night with her, she was speechless.

"Sarah, I thought you were deceased. Everyone looked and looked for you after your divorce and no one could find you. You look wonderful. Where are you living now?"

Sarah glanced quickly around the room hoping Ed had been detained much longer with his business. Finally, finding her voice and her manners, and not knowing what to say, she told Florence to sit down. "I'm so happy to see you," she lied.

Giving Florence a quick rundown on her life in Chicago for the last few years she tried to remain calm and at the same time keep her eyes out for Ed.

"Right now I've been stood up by a friend who was supposed to meet me hours ago for dinner. I need to go back to my room and get some work done. The next time I'm in New York. I'll give you a call and we'll have lunch."

"I can't wait. I'm so glad to have found you. Please hurry back and let's do have lunch."

Sarah left the dining room just in time to catch Ed coming in the lobby of the hotel.

"Quick, Ed. We have to get out of here." Sarah grabbed his arm and shoved him into the elevator car.

"What's going on?"

"It's Florence. She is here meeting a friend for dinner. She found me waiting in the dining room.

The couple went up to Sarah's room, but the evening was spoiled for both of them. For the first time Sarah thought only of Florence and how horrible for her it would be if she ever found out about Ed's affair. If Florence knew one of her former best friends and her husband were together it would devastate her. Sarah quickly put that thought in the very back of her consciousness.

Ed wanted to carefully plan the next day so there would be no chance his wife would be able to interfere. Leaving Sarah to ponder the itinerary for tomorrow, Ed sneaked out of the hotel by the back way.

The next evening after their close call with Florence in the Biltmore, Ed thought they needed a financial discussion. Settling into a private booth in a small restaurant in "Little Italy" for a quick dinner before going to the theater, Ed broached the subject of financial independence.

"You are aware money is the reason I couldn't leave Florence years ago…and, oh yes, the children. Perrine is in college now and Gwen is almost eighteen. You know we could still be married if we built up a nest egg again. Do you think we should invest in stocks? I'm doing really well right now in the market."

Sarah contemplated. They had done nicely in stocks and bonds before. Some of the money she had started the shop with had come from Ed when he liquidated their old account and sent the proceeds to her. Both of them had been exceptionally good at picking stocks that would increase in value.

The waiter came by their booth and dropped off two plates of linguini which usually got Sarah's immediate attention. Not tonight however. She was deep in thought remembering that Ed once before had said that lack of money was keeping them apart. He had told her there was not enough money in their stock account to allow him to leave his wife who controlled his purse strings.

Ignoring her dinner she finally said, "I'm not going to believe in that 'marriage' line again, but maybe the stock market would be a good idea. It could pay for my visits to New York and your visits here."

"We have been so happy these last couple of years and both of us have grown to be better individuals. Let's try to make money again, and please don't give up on me this time. I think we can still be together legally for the rest of our lives," said Ed.

Florence's image flited across Sarah's mind, but after a moment Sarah thoughtfully replied, "I have a great deal of money between the shop and my land. The market is probably the safest place I could put it right now. It's performing unbelievably. Let's do it. When you get back to New York buy me 100 shares of RCA. It's up to $400.00 a share now and climbing daily."

Their usual discussion followed with Ed finally saying, "I believe RCA is overpriced now, but for you I'll buy it. For my part I'll buy DuPont. It's over $200.00 a share, and it's a really stable company."

Feeling she could trust Ed, Sarah relaxed with the thought of making more money than she could on her own and maybe a marriage proposal to go along with the riches.

She slowly but happily downed her cold linguini.

CHAPTER 26

Dream Voyage

Switzerland 1928

Sarah fidgeted in her desk chair at the shop. "Nancy, I know my figures are right, but I can hardly believe them. My ledger shows our profits have doubled in just the last month. Unbelievable... I'm going to get a raise and so are you."

Nancy stopped pricing the batch of hats that Elizabeth had dropped off and said, "Unbelievable is the right word. I never dreamed we would do so well. A raise sounds wonderful to me. Sadie, you are so successful."

Closing the ledger, Sarah looked around the big room full of hats. The S & E Millinery Shop with Elizabeth's help had become a destination for many women all over the country. *Yes, I am successful. I am wealthy. My properties are bringing in good rent, the investment account that Ed and I jointly own is growing by leaps and bounds. I am seeing the love of my life frequently and Ruby brings sunshine into my life on most week-ends.*

Although Ed did come to Chicago on a bimonthly schedule, he mentioned that Florence was getting suspicious of his time away from New York even to the point of calling his employer to make sure he was traveling on business. Covering his tracks with believable excuses to do jobs for the company in Chicago and occasionally taking time out to do some work, he performed well for Piedmont Electric. Therefore, they told Florence "yes" he worked hard for them in Chicago and other places out-of-town as well.

The phone rang as Sarah sat dreaming of her wealth. "I'll get it, Nancy."

Ed's voice came booming over the line, "Happy New Year, my dear Sallie. We missed the celebration to usher in 1928 together, but I have something to make up for that. Get your passport ready to go to London. I have business there and would be traveling alone unless you will go with me."

"What a great way for us to celebrate the New Year since we couldn't manage being together during the holidays. Of course I'll go with you" Sarah declared.

That night she quickly began sorting out the clothes she would take on the London trip.

However, two days later Ed called and said, "I'm so sorry but my business trip has been postponed. The Thames River flooded and destroyed the home office of the company I was to visit. But…I knew you would be disappointed so I have already arranged another trip abroad for us. We are going to Switzerland for the Olympic Games in February."

"I don't know whether to be happy or sad. Guess I'll have to be both. Seriously though, I am thrilled. I want to see the Olympic Games and I've always wanted to go to Switzerland," said Sarah.

The extra month she now had gave her plenty of time to pack and make her arrangements for Elizabeth and Nancy to run the shop while she would be gone. Every day she spent many hours just looking forward to a wonderful trip with the love of her life, Ed.

On February fourth they boarded the ship that was to take them to Europe and Sarah had a surprise. She did not feel good as they settled into their stateroom on the luxury ship. *Am I ill? What is the matter with me?*

Ed was worried, "Are you getting sick from the motion of the boat before we even sail?"

"I don't know. I suddenly don't feel well."

"It's been a rush to get ready for the trip and get on the boat. Just lie down on the bed and rest for a while. I'll go see if I can find you a snack of some sort," said a concerned Ed.

Sarah did as she was told and Ed left the stateroom. Her eyes darted around their state- room. She saw an image not of the beautiful place surrounding her, but of the area her family had occupied on a ship when they left Norway. She experienced first tossing and turning on a small ship to Liverpool, then boarding a big ship and settling in a place called "steerage" to cross the ocean to get to America. It was 1883 again and she was a child. The memory of that trip came flooding back to her in giant waves.

She remembered every detail of the twenty-one days on the ocean. The smell! *That's why I feel sick. What makes the stink? Oh, God! There must have been a hundred people in that room. We were not allowed out of the place except for maybe an hour in the afternoon on a good day. If there was a storm, we couldn't go outside at all. Our family of five had two cots to sleep on. I slept with one of my sisters and Mom slept with the other. Father didn't have a cot but he couldn't sleep anyway because he had to keep our luggage by our side and keep other people's luggage from hitting us as it rolled across the floor with the ship's motion. One meal a day was given to us but everyone who ate it usually got sick. A bad storm came and we were not allowed outside the room for two whole days. I have a vivid memory of the day we were again permitted outside. For an extra-long time we watched while the ship's crew threw things overboard. At the time I didn't know what those things were. I now know they were people's bodies.*

Ed came back in the room with some crackers and a soda. "Here, Sallie, drink this."

"Oh, Ed, I'm not ill sick. I'm just upset remembering what it was like on the ship bringing my family to America. It was a horror show. Now here I am traveling in luxury, but I can't forget the first trip I had on the ocean. I don't know how many people in our big room died, but there were a lot of them. Conditions were terrible. Tell me that there isn't such a thing as "steerage" on this ship."

"No, there isn't any steerage on this ship or any other passenger ship today. That's a thing of the past. People's lifes have improved so much since you came here as a child. The world has made great strides in health care, machinery, education, and you name it. Don't transport yourself back to harder times. Get dressed and let's go see what the ship has to offer."

Sarah managed to shake off her horrible memories and dressed in her perkiest outfit to begin getting acquainted with the ship.

The rest of their voyage was enjoyed in beautiful weather and without incident. Upon arriving in Switzerland the happy couple took a hike up the side of a small mountain after checking into their hotel.

"I am so excited to be in St. Moritz and actually get to watch all the sports. I can't wait to see the figure skating. I read where Sonja Henie, who by the way is from Norway like me, is expected to be in competition for the gold medal. I'm so happy Florence didn't want to come with you.

What is your favorite sport? I'll bet the skiing will be your favorite," Sarah chatted on sounding more like a child than a mature woman.

Every day they spent most of the time watching the spectacular games, but managed to break away to also absorb some the Swiss culture. They really enjoyed watching the cows on the mountainside and learning some of the customs of the Swiss people.

"Have you noticed that the natives open their bedroom windows each morning no matter how cold it is? They air out their bedding and breathe in the fresh air. I think I'll do that when I return home," declared Sarah.

Sonja Henie did win the gold medal in figure skating, making the trip perfect for Sarah. "I have never been so happy in all my life."

On the ship ride home she tried to sort out her life with Ed. *I sound like Madame Lily but I believe it was ordained that Ed and I are not to be married. I don't believe that we could be as happy with each other as we are today. If we shared the monotony of everyday life, our lives would not be so perfect. Right now we each get to do our own thing and go our own way. Ed says he feels soon we will have enough money in our stock account for him to leave Florence and marry me. I believe I am happy just the way things are. What a change. I find I like being free and having a soul mate. I am looking forward to going home alone, back to Chicago.*

CHAPTER 27

Disaster

Chicago, Illinois 1929

Sarah had successfully put her former life behind her but still dreamed of making a trip to Decatur to see her friend June and visit Sam's grave. Telling herself she didn't believe in the forewarning from the stars, she still fretted when she thought of Madame Lily's warning of death should she return.

I'm not going to worry about predictions. I am going to Decatur. At this point I'm sure I don't have to worry about William. I'll call Ed and tell him to postpone his trip to see me this month because I'm going to Decatur.

Sarah telephoned Ed at work to tell him of her plans. "Hello, Ed. Don't plan on a visit this month because I'm planning to finally go back to Decatur to visit my Sam's grave and see June. I'll miss you deeply, but I need to do this. It's been eight years since I left. Surely I don't have to worry about William anymore and I do miss my trips to the cemetery. You, Sam, and June are the only people I truly care about."

"I'll miss you. You know my life revolves around my visits with you. However, missing my trip to Chicago will help my credibility with Florence. She is getting more and more suspicious about my trips. In fact, I'm worried that she might try to follow me. When are you going?"

"I'm planning to be there on Halloween. Sam always loved the fall and was especially fond of Halloween night. I'll probably stay with June if she'll have me after all this time. I hope she'll understand why I haven't been in touch with her."

"June will recognize that you feared what William would do if he found you. Do be careful of him. I don't think he will harm you now, but stay out of his way. He was shocked to see you a few years ago in the Palmer House. But, since then he has remarried and become President of Faries Manufacturing. I don't think he is bothered by you at this point. Just be careful of who you see and where you go," said Ed.

"I am planning to leave on the twenty-fourth, stay through Halloween, and come home on November first."

Sarah made arrangements to be gone from her shop for a week and asked her friend Elizabeth to take care of her apartment while she was gone. Sarah talked to Ruby who was a happy girl now that she had a pretend mother and made arrangements to have her spend the week-end with Elizabeth. Just one more thing to do and that was to go see Madame Lily.

I am going no matter what Madame Lily says, but I hope she gives me a good forecast for my trip.

On October twenty-second Sarah stopped packing for the trip and went to see Madame Lily. Upon entering the clairvoyant's oppressive room, Sarah felt chills. She almost turned around and left.

No. Madame Lily has been right about everything in my life up till now. I have to hear what she has to say.

Sarah sat in the big overstuffed chair and prepared to hear her future.

Madame Lily stared into her crystal ball and after a moment said, "I see disaster coming into your life. You will lose the handsome man you are with and at the same time lose all your money. You are planning a trip. If you go, you will not survive."

Sarah was angry. "Why are you tormenting me like this? My life cannot turn that bad."

"I only tell you what I see. It's in the stars."

Sarah huffed out of Madame Lily's parlor. She was about two miles from her apartment but decided she needed to walk to vent her anger. Taking off on a fast pace she dug her heels into the sidewalk as she marched trying to calm her emotional upset. *The predictions of disaster couldn't be true. She would call Ed when she got home.*

Luckily Ed was available when she called. Her thoughts tumbled out and didn't come in logical order. "Tell me that you love me. How is our money doing in the stock market? Don't you think a trip to Decatur would be good for me?"

"Slow down, Sarah. What is the matter?"

"I went to see Madame Lily and she told me all sorts of horrible things. She said I was going to lose you and all my money. Also, I shouldn't go on my trip because I would die if I did."

"Don't pay attention to her, Sarah. I love you and I think a trip to your former home would be great .She might be closer to the truth about our money, but we aren't going to lose it all. The market is losing a little of its shine, but I think it will recover," said Ed.

"I'm glad you think I should keep my plans for my trip. I will go. I don't like to hear your assessment of the markets however because at this point all my money is there. I've even sold most of my property and put the money our stock account."

"Don't worry. It will turn around. Get some sleep tonight. All is well. Enjoy your trip."

Sarah finished her packing and slept well that night. Ed was right ...all was well. She spent the next day getting her shop ready to function without her. In two days she would be on the train to Decatur. Madame Lily's forecast became a distant memory.

About 9:30 the night before her trip, she was in her bedroom looking in the closet trying to decide whether or not to pack one more outfit into her already overflowing trunk. The phone rang. *Great it would be Ed.* As she answered, the sound of his voice told her something was terribly wrong.

"Sallie, I love you dearly... I ...don't know how to tell you this," sputtered Ed.

Sarah braced herself knowing by his tone something awful had happened. Sitting down in the bedroom chair to prepare for the worst, she asked in a soft voice, "Are you ill?" "

"Yes but not from physical causes...Sarah, we have lost all of the money we put into the stock market."

Not knowing whether to be relieved or upset, Sarah replied, "I'm glad you're not sick.

Sarah and Ed were both silent for a moment. Sarah found her voice, "What do you mean 'all of our money'? The stocks always go up and down, but they do recover."

"I'm afraid they won't this time. This is a disastrous crash. We are broke. Men are committing suicide, jumping out windows. It's awful."

Sarah found it difficult to accept what Ed was saying. If it were true, she would be broke. She had sold most of her property and put all of the store's profits into the growing stock market.

Trying to end the conversation on a positive note, she declared. "It can't be as bad as you think. Get some sleep and we will know more in the morning."

After a sleepless night she went to the neighborhood drugstore and bought a Chicago Tribune the next morning. It was true. The market had had its biggest crash in its history. Men were jumping out of windows to commit suicide. It would be doubtful if they had much money left.

Steeling herself against what she knew was going to be true, she phoned Ed. "Okay. Talk to me. What do we have left?"

"Virtually nothing I'm afraid. It's partially my fault. I was buying on margin lately because the market was doing so well. That only compounds the problem now as we have to pay back what I borrowed. It kills me to have to tell you this, but by my calculations we only have about 300 hundred dollars left in our account."

Ed fell silent for moment then said in a very soft voice, "I love you so, Sallie. I don't know how to make it better, but I will work my hands to the bone to get you back the money you put into the account."

She had put in thousands and thousands of dollars. Really all she had. *Now I'm broke!* Her trip was off. For one thing she couldn't afford it right now and for another thing Madame Lily was again right about what was to happen in her life. Considering the astrologist's whole reading it made Sarah nervous to consider going to Decatur.

As reality set in she walked into her kitchen and took her frustration out against the only thing she could. She picked up one of her prettiest plates and threw it with vengeance against the wall smashing it to pieces. Picking up the chards of broken glass that were all over the floor, she cut herself. Blood spilled on the floor reminding her of the hopelessness of her actions.

CHAPTER 28

Broke

Fall 1929

After two sleepless nights, Sarah got out of bed and became aware that she had not dressed or bathed for several days. *What is the word I want for how I feel…despair. I have to face my situation.* She wanted support from her soul mate, but after her initial panic she had realized Ed couldn't come to Chicago because he had to attempt to solve his own financial problems. She was alone.

In the middle of the afternoon she was sitting outside in a comfortable Adirondacks chair trying to relax when her practical side began nagging at her to get up and do something. She should be working at the shop instead of gazing around at the lovely scene.

The sun shone brightly on the mums and other fall flowers that were still colorful but starting to fade. A gentle breeze blew the blossoms back and forth creating the illusion they were dancing. Sitting in this calm and beautiful setting, Sarah couldn't entertain the idea of just giving up. But she needed help. Although she had not been very religious since Sam died, she decided God might still be willing to help her.

God, I need you. I know how bad I've been, but I want to try and be a morally upright woman now. Please help me out of this mess. I promise I will be a good Christian.

As she looked around the beautiful garden at God's handy work, she felt he was giving her an answer. *Don't give up. Many of the flowers you are enjoying today are dying, but... they will be back next year just as beautiful as they are now. They will just be out of sight for a while gathering strength.*

Sarah felt much better. She knew what to do. It was going to be difficult but she would do the right thing. First, give Ed back to Florence. As a couple she and Ed enjoyed and loved each other, but he shouldn't hurt his family. No matter that Ed was her one and only real love, it wasn't meant to be. Madame Lily was right. She would lose her handsome male partner. He was morally obligated to take care of his family. *Ed will object outwardly, but inside he too will know it has to be.* Sarah needed to have the strength to break up their affair. God said.

Ed called the next day. "I am sending you $150.00. I'm so sorry but that's half of what I was able to get out of our account."

Disregarding the financial news she had just received, Sarah tried to imagine that Ed was not the person on the other end of the phone line. That didn't work. In her mind she could see Ed and knew he was as upset as she was. Breathing deeply so as not to pass out, she finally spoke in a husky voice believing God had told her what to say. "We can never see each other ever again, Ed. I want you to take care of Florence and your children. You and I know that our love will last forever, but we can't see each other. Don't even write. You know this is the way it has to be."

Ed was silent for a long minute but finally said, "I know what I have to do." Another minute of silence. "Maybe things will change some time in the future. I can't bear to think of never seeing you again." More silence. "I'll try to send you some money whenever I can. If you are ever in trouble call me to help you."

"Good-bye, Ed. I love you dearly."

Sarah hung up the phone. Luckily she was sitting in a chair because her legs wouldn't hold her up. She sat trying to make peace with what she had done feeling very sad and lonely. She grieved for her relationship, but she had made her pact with God.

No one can take away the memories I have of my time with Ed. Although we didn't see each other daily, we wrote letters practically every day. In total we had almost nine joyful years together. I'll live with the thoughts of that. Many married couples often don't even have that much time together.

After a sleepless night Sarah turned her attention to the S & E Millinery Shop the next day. With all her excess money gone she now had to count on the shop for her living expenses. But week after week Sarah noticed the volume of shoppers for her hats became slimmer and slimmer. She had to lay off two of her clerks keeping only Nancy who had been with her from the beginning. The ladies, who had purchased as many hats as they wanted, now had to control their spending. It seemed like everyone was devastated by the market crash.

With her shop beginning to fail she considered what her options might be. Most of her property she had sold to put the money in the stock market. How about the money William had given her from the divorce settlement which she had never claimed? Sarah was sure that had been given back to him after seven years when she would have been declared legally dead and she was equally sure he never bothered to tell Sarah's attorney that she was alive after he discovered her in Chicago.

I would never take money from William. That is my contribution for the way I treated him before the divorce. He was a bad husband, but at the end I was a bad wife. That's why I left him all my assets in my will. I guess now I might not have anything left when I die.

The situation only got worse. After several months of trying to get the rent from the little bit of property she had left, she realized her renters couldn't pay and she didn't have money for her taxes. When the bills came in, she lost ownership of all her land.

The situation became drastic, so bad that she even considered turning to her first husband. Good old Charles. He had been the unfaithful one in their marriage cheating on her with one of his client's daughters. He owed her.

As she considered whether or not to contact Charles Elwood (Sam's father), Elizabeth, who was vacationing in the west, sent her several articles from the Seattle Daily Times. Sarah felt the articles were timely.

The first article headline read: WIFE 'SHIELDING' HUSBAND, IS HER COURT TESTIMONY

The paper goes on to quote the wife saying: "I am suing for separation instead of divorce to save my husband, to save him from himself. I am sorry for him. I am doing this because I once loved him dearly, because I believe that the man I married twenty-seven years ago has died. The man I married was kind, and sweet, and trustworthy and he wouldn't have hurt me for anything in the world."

As Sarah read on she couldn't help but giggle. Her former husband was anything but trustworthy and she believed he was incapable of truly loving anyone.

Clara, his present wife, the person Charles had cheated on with Sarah, went on to say: "This man is only his shadow. But I want to take care of him, to shield him from others. That is why I am suing only for separate maintenance instead of divorce."

Enjoying the article thoroughly, Sarah couldn't help but feel happy that Charles was finally getting slammed in court for doing what he did to her years before. According to the Times, "On the witness stand Clara attributed their present estrangement after more than a decade of unusually happy married life to his infatuation with a married woman, Mrs. Caroline Anderson, wife of Herbert Anderson…a brass molder."

"Anderson sat in court and swung his foot unconcernedly over the arm of a chair as he heard Mrs. Elwood relate that on two occasions her husband allegedly broke down and hysterically confessed his love for the brass molder's wife. He laughed when Mrs. Elwood's attorney…produced in court the original of a release given Elwood by Anderson, in which the latter gave written promise for a consideration not to sue him for alienation of affections."

Elizabeth also enclosed in her letter an article written in the paper two days later giving the outcome of the trial. The headline of the second article read: MRS. ELWOOD GIVEN DIVORCE AND SHARE OF $97,000 ESTATE.

This article stated that Mrs. Elwood was granted a divorce and awarded a share of the community property said to be less than offered her before the trial by her husband. The judge declared that he was not granting the divorce based on Mrs. Elwood's allegations of her husband's relationship with Mrs. Anderson, a grandmother.

Sarah stopped giggling as she realized that Charles would not be able to help her out of her financial problem either.

After ignoring my family for years, I can't go to them for help now. For years she had not tried to contact her parents or siblings. In fact, she did not even know who might be alive or dead at this time. She had distanced herself from them when she became Mrs. William Grady, a society woman of great stature. She was alone.

My shop is going under. I can no longer pay my bills. I can't even afford to stay in my apartment. What Madame Lily said is coming true. I wonder if she can tell me what to do?

Sarah closed her shop for the day and decided to walk home. Depression was setting in. Maybe a walk would clear her mind and show her what to do.

CHAPTER 29

Solutions

Chicago, Illinois 1931

Sarah had never been in a situation where hard work and determination couldn't solve the problem. And she had a problem... that was unsolvable. Every day in her mail there were more bills, more bad news.

After months of not being able to pay her mortgage on the shop and taxes on her property, the courts began taking everything away from her. The government took not only her building but also the inventory to help pay for Sarah's delinquent months. She couldn't even pay the lease on her apartment.

Sarah took temporary help from Elizabeth so she could stay another month in the apartment. Most of her nice jewelry she took to a pawn shop to get enough money to buy food. The small amount of money coming from Ed was an attempt to help her but insufficient to even buy groceries.

I have to make some money. I've never had this problem before.

After some introspection, Sarah decided on a solution. *Sarah Petersen Elwood Grady you are a smart business woman with some talent. You are going to have to find a job.*

After an unproductive morning, Sarah sat in her rocking chair by the picture window looking out over the garden. She watched as two squirrels played "ring around the rosie" on the trunk of a large elm tree.

Finally deciding, rather than sitting all afternoon daydreaming in the apartment she was about to lose, she would be better off getting some exercise and taking a walk outside. She still cared how she looked to the public so she put on one of her nicer hats and a sweater that coordinated with her dress. Passing a mirror on her way out, she adjusted her hair and complimented herself on her appearance. *At least I look good.*

Walking several blocks from the apartment she entered a commercial zone. *Why is there such a huge line of people standing in front of that building? Where did they come from?*

As Sarah walked closer she became well aware what these people were doing. They were standing in line to get food. She recognized one man who was fairly well dressed as the husband of one of the ladies who used to regularly buy hats from her shop. The reality of the depression of the whole country came crashing down on her. *I am certainly not the only one suffering right now. I have to get a job.* After deciding to spend some of her very limited funds on a Chicago Tribune, she almost ran home with her newspaper.

In the relatively safe and quiet environment of the apartment, she opened the Tribune to the want ads in the classified section. The help wanted section seemed very small. Just as she was proclaiming she shouldn't have purchased the paper, her eyes landed on one ad:

WOMAN WANTED

DOMESTIC HELP

FAMILY WITH ONE CHILD

CALL SAGINAW 5094

Sarah read and reread the ad several times. *Why not? I certainly have experience with domestic help even if it was on the other side. I like children. It's worth a phone call.*

She picked up the phone receiver with determination and dialed the number. "Hello. My name is Sarah Grady. I am a widow. In answer to your ad, I'm very experienced in domestic affairs."

Widow sounds better than divorcee. " Presently I am looking for work."

"How much experience have you had in running a household?" asked the woman on the other end of the line.

"I ran a large estate for twenty years." *Well that's true. It was my house but it was the same thing.*

"How old are you?"

Oh oh. Now what do I say? I guess I'll have to be as truthful as I can. "I am around fifty. I don't know exactly because I was born in Norway and don't have a birth certificate. I am in very good health."

"You are Norwegian? So is our family. My name is Hilde Olsen. I would like to talk to you in person. If you are interested in the job come to 824 Kenmore Boulevard at ten o'clock tomorrow and we will discuss the job."

Sarah hung up the phone. *What have I done? From the number one socialite in Decatur, Illinois, to the owner of an extremely successful millinery shop in Chicago, now I am to be someone's maid...if they'll have me.*

She felt like crying, but realized that would do no good. Swallowing her pride she looked in her closet to see what outfit would make her look younger and like a wonderful maid.

159

The next morning she fought off her nervousness and got dressed for her interview. She wanted to bolt and run… but managed to control her emotions and arrive at the Olsen house at exactly ten o'clock.

The house, she noted, had many similarities to her Millikin Place home. It was shingle style with a California flavor. She rang the huge brass bell on the door and took deep breaths while she waited.

The door opened revealing an attractive woman probably in her late thirties. She looked like a Norwegian, tall, slender, and blonde. As she smiled she held out her hand and said, "Hi. I'm Hilde."

Also smiling Sarah began to relax and stated, "I am Sarah Grady."

"Do come in Sarah and sit while we discuss the job." Hilde took Sarah into the living room and motioned for her to take a seat. "First could I offer you a cup of tea?"

"Yes, I would love one." *This will give me a chance to look around the room while she's in the kitchen.*

As soon as Hilde left the room, Sarah began examining the surroundings. Some of the furnishings like the couch were Victorian, but the chairs and tables were Arts and Crafts. They had been put together well so the impression of the room was comfortable and agreeable. *So far so good, but I've got to straighten that crooked picture. It spoils the entire impression of the room.*

Sarah got up from her chair and straightened the picture just as Hilde came back into the room.

Hilde presented the tea and stated, "I see you are bothered by my favorite floral picture hanging askew on the wall. It upsets me too. Thanks for straightening it, but in about five minutes it will hang crooked again. "

The women made small talk as they drank their tea. Hilde made a comment that she thought Sarah was accustomed to being a station above a house maid, but she knew times were difficult for everyone. The former socialite simply continued to sip her tea.

Hilde's tone became serious as she said to Sarah, "I need someone who will become part of the family, help clean the house, be a companion to my ten year old daughter Ingrid, and manage our other employees. I have a cook and a laundress but no other help right now. I can offer you fifteen dollars a week and a nice two room suite on the third floor to live in. I am impressed you felt impelled to straighten a picture and believe you would make a fine addition to our home.

Sarah cringed at the thought of living on fifteen dollars a week. But on the plus side she realized this job would give her a place to stay and a little money in addition. Having nowhere else to go and judging the family she would become a part of as upright and Christian, she mustered as much enthusiasm as she could and said, "I would be delighted to serve your family."

Getting ready to go out the front door Sarah turned and asked, "Would it be alright if I had a child visit me sometimes on week –ends? She is younger than your Ingrid but I think Ingrid might enjoy her company. Her name is Ruby."

"What a pretty name. I think it would do Ingrid good to have another child around, especially if she would be the older and wiser one," said Hilde.

CHAPTER 30

Family Life

Chicago, Illinois 1932

"Ingrid, hurry up or you will be late for school," said Sarah trying to bring calm to the moment. "Do take your rain coat and boots. It's raining cats and dogs."

"If it were really raining cats and dogs, I'd go get one and bring it into the house. Sarah, why won't Mother and Father let me have a dog?" asked Ingrid.

"Oh, for heaven's sake. Get your coat on and go. You don't want to be tardy."

As Ingrid slammed the front door, Sarah sat down to have her morning cup of tea. Her thoughts raced back to Decatur when Sam had come to live with her and William permanently. At that time he had been about four years older than Ingrid was now. He too had begged for a dog and was denied. *William said I didn't have time to take care of a dog and he couldn't trust Sam to take on that responsibility. Oh how I wish Sam could have gotten the pet he wanted.*

Ingrid was such a sweet and loving child. Sarah hated to see her wanting something that might be in Sarah's power to give. *If I spoke to Hilde about getting a dog, I think she might agree. I'll try to do that today.*

Sarah felt like Ingrid was the grandchild she never had. A horrible set of circumstances had brought her to the John Olsen's home almost eight months ago. However, now she had never been happier. John, Hilde, and Ingrid were her family and they had accepted Ruby as a welcome frequent visitor. Ingrid loved Ruby like a sister.

The third floor of the house bore many similarities to her Millikin Place home in Decatur and the space was all hers. The weekends were her own when she had something to do. Her salary had been raised to twenty dollars a week, but best of all she adored the family and they in turn loved her.

Hilde drifted downstairs, "Good Morning, Sarah. I see Ingrid got off to school all right. Sometimes I'm not sure whether it's you or Ingrid that is leaving…or both. What confusion."

From the beginning of Sarah's tenure Hilde had insisted that she be addressed only as "Hilde". After all she had said "we are family".

Sarah saw her opportunity to bring up the subject of a family dog. "I need to ask you something, Hilde. Would you be terribly against having a pet in the house?"

Hilde responded, "Who wants a dog…Ingrid or you?"

"Well, Ingrid of course. But I wouldn't mind one. Remember I came from a farm where we always had animals. I believe a pet is good for children. It teaches them to love, to be unselfish, and to respect others. Ingrid and I would have the care of him…"

"Oh, all right. It's two against one. I know when I am beaten. Make sure the dog is a 'him'. I don't want babies."

Sarah immediately began her search for the perfect pet. It took two days, but she finally found what she considered to be the one for Ingrid. It was an eighteen month old, rust colored, male Cocker Spaniel named "Rusty" who was already trained to use the outside bathroom.

Rusty arrived at the house about two o'clock in the afternoon so he would be there to greet Ingrid when she returned from school. She came home from school as usual a little after three. Upon opening the door she saw the dog who greeted her warmly. Immediately the two of them were wrestling around on the floor in playful combat.

Finally Ingrid came up for air. "Whose dog is this, Sarah? He's beautiful."

"Happy early birthday. He's yours, but don't hug him so tightly or you'll hurt him."

"Oh, thank you, thank you. This is the best day of my life."

"Mine too," was all Sarah could say as she fought back the tears. The Olsen's were the family she never had... except when she was growing up. How blessed she was now.

Sarah's happiness triggered her nostalgia for returning to Decatur to see June and visit her son's grave. In addition to her new family; Ruby, Elizabeth, Ed, June, and Sam were the only people in her life that she wanted to remember. The last chapter had been written on Ed after the stock market crash when they both realized that he needed to take care of his legal family. She loved him dearly but knew she would never be able to see him again.

As she thought about June and Sam's grave, she determined that she had to go to Decatur. Her life would never be complete until she visited them again. But every time she tried to make plans for a trip, Madame Lily's prediction came creeping back into her mind.

Coming back into the moment, Sarah realized she needed to make arrangements for the cook to add dog food to the grocery list and she needed to fashion a bed for Rusty. The bed ideally should be in Ingrid's room, but Hilde must be consulted before making that happen. Sarah left the happy duo on the floor in the reception hall and went to take care of business.

The idea of making a trip back into her past was still in the fore front of her mind. She would have to consult Madame Lily again. Maybe the stars would have a brighter outcome this time.

CHAPTER 31

To Go or Not To Go

Chicago, Illinois 1933

No matter how wonderful the situation remained with her new family, Sarah's thoughts of making a trip to Decatur wouldn't disappear. She needed an opinion from Madame Lily. Sarah tried hard to remember when the astrologer had been incorrect about events in her life. Not one thing came to mind. Therefore, she could not dismiss the fear she had about the Madame's last prophecy. She had to hear the prediction again.

"Hilde, I need to run an errand, but I'll be back before Ingrid gets home from school."

"That's fine. I'll be here all afternoon anyway."

Sarah hopped on the streetcar that would deliver her just a half a block from the clairvoyant's residence. *No matter what she says I have to hear it.* Her steps slowed as she got off the car and walked to Madame Lily's house which also was her place of business. An appointment was not needed, but sometimes Sarah had to wait if the Madame was reading for others.

Today was a waiting day. The door to the reading room was closed meaning Madame Lily was busy. Sarah sat in the straight backed chair with nothing but her own thoughts to distract her. And they did distract her. *I don't really believe the stars know more about my life than I do. If*

I want to go to Decatur, I should just go. Some garishly dressed woman shouldn't be able to tell me what to do. I need to get out of this place, go home to my family where I belong, and make plans for the trip I want.

At that minute a well- dressed matronly woman came out of the room nodding to Sarah as she quickly left the house. Madame Lily appeared in the doorway of her private room and motioned for Sarah to come in. Sarah had all but decided that she would not go in and hear what Madame had to say, but found herself walking into the place where she was about to hear her fate.

The den, as Sarah called it, hadn't changed since her last visit. The ceiling, walls, and probably windows were still draped with black and red velvet material making the room very dark. In the middle of the room sat a large round table that held the crystal ball, several stacks of cards, and other things that Sarah could not define.

"Please be seated and I will tell you soon what the stars have in store for you," said Madame Lily in a hushed voice not seeming to acknowledge Sarah had been there many times before. "Is there something you specifically want to know about?"

"Of course. I need to know how the trip I'm planning will turn out," replied Sarah.

Madame Lily went into her silent routine and looked into the crystal ball. Next, without speaking, she took a stack of cards and began to turn them over.

"I know this is not what you want to hear but I have to tell you what is in the stars… and they are always right," said the stern clairvoyant. "All my sources are telling me the same thing. If you go on the trip that you desire, you will not return. You will die!"

167

"That is so unbelievable. How do you see me dying? Do I get sick? Does someone kill me? Is there an accident? Be more specific please."

"I cannot give you details. All I see is death when you are away on a trip. The stars have told us."

Madame Lily got up from her chair signaling that the session was over. Sarah tingled with anger. What could she do? Madame was not going to change her predictions so Sarah could either believe them or not. The upsetting reading left her a bit unhinged, but she had the presence of mind to pay for her session and get away from the house.

I can't go home I don't want the Olsens to see me when I'm so upset. How can I calm down when I have a prophecy like this?

She took a different streetcar that would take her to Elizabeth. Luckily for Sarah her loyal friend was home.

"Sorry to come unannounced, but I have to talk to someone who knows me and my ancient circumstances."

Elizabeth questioned, "What do you mean by 'ancient circumstances'?"

"You know… someone who is familiar with my life in Decatur. I know I'm not making much sense, but I just came from Madame Lily and I'm terribly upset. Her prediction is that if I go to Decatur I will die."

"Oh, Sarah, that's horrible. What made her say that?"

"The stars. She insists that the stars have ordained this outcome if I make the trip."

Both women sat quietly for a few minutes taking stock of the prediction. Finally Elizabeth spoke, "I think you should not go. Madame Lily is usually right in her assessment of what the stars ordain."

Sarah jumped into the conversation. "Have you ever known her to be wrong?"

Elizabeth disregarded Sarah's question, "In light of what you have been told, you must make a decision. Is it worth the risk to go?"

"You are ignoring my question, but I know the answer. I was wrong to bring you into this problem with me. It is my decision. As Shakespeare would say 'To go or not to go…that is the question'." And it's my question."

Sarah went home sorry she had brought Elizabeth into her problem. *I have wrestled with this for years. I'm going to forget the prophesy of that astrologer and do what I want to do which is go to Decatur to visit June and Sam's grave .Madame Lily doesn't know everything. I'm going to check with Hilde and see when she can do without me for a few days.*

CHAPTER 32

The Trip

Decatur, Illinois 1933

Sarah sat at her desk. She realized she was sweating. *What do you say to your best friend that you haven't been in contact with for twelve years who also thinks you're dead?* Feeling pushed by some exterior force, she picked up the phone, dialed O for the long distance operator, and waited. Her hands shook and her mouth was dry. *How will June react to my call? She thinks I'm dead. I should have called her before now. I...*

The long distance operator broke into Sarah's thoughts. "Number please."

"I need Decatur, Illinois 4390."

After what seemed like an eternity. June Johns answered her phone. "Hello."

Sarah opened her mouth but nothing came out.

"Hello," June repeated.

Sarah tried again and succeeded in blurting out, "June, it's Sarah."

"Who?"

"Sarah."

No sound from June.

Sarah found her normal voice, "It's Sarah Grady."

Another pause, but finally June began to get excited. "Is it really you, Sarah? It sounds a bit like you… but I thought you were deceased. No one has heard from you for years. Where have you been? I have so many questions."

Sarah replied after a minute, "It's me, June and I'd like to plan a trip to Decatur. I want to see you and visit Sam's grave. I can fill you in on my life these last twelve years when I come."

"Sarah, Sarah Grady. It's really you. I'm so happy. You sound like you're OK. Come and stay with Corwin and me…any time. I can't wait."

"Me either. I'd love to stay with you. Would it be alright if I came next Friday?"

"Wonderful. Where are you coming from? I could meet your train, or are you driving?"

At that point an image crossed Sarah's mind of the fashion model she always had been when she lived in Decatur and had money, and a car. She would be a bit ashamed to go to her former home in her present outfits, but decided June wouldn't care. However, she really didn't want to run into anyone else. She would find a way to get to June's house without any fanfare.

"I'm coming from Chicago, probably by train, but don't worry about getting me from the station. I'm not sure whether I'll be on the early or late train. I'll take a taxi. I don't want to see anyone except you and, of course, Corwin."

"I can hardly believe it's you. I'll be so excited to see you," said June.

Sarah hung up the phone. It had been wonderful to hear June's voice, but at the same time she was distraught. Many good memories flew through her mind, but at the same time so many bad memories overwhelmed them.

Sarah gave herself one of her famous pep talks. *I will not back down to the ghost of William, Madame Lily, or anyone else that tries to keep me from going to Decatur. Even if I do die, as is foreordained, I will have connected with my son when I visit his grave and I will get to be with my best friend who I dearly love.*

With determination she pulled out her trunk from her bedroom closet and began to pack. Wishing she had the means to buy a new outfit, she decided her hat, which was relatively new from her shop, would have to make the rest of her look good.

Ingrid came into her room and asked, "Where are you going?"

"I'm going back to a place where I used to live and visit with some people."

"When are you going? You know my birthday party is in fourteen days. You have to be here."

"Oh, I'll be back in plenty of time for your party."

"Can I go with you?" said Ingrid as she jumped up on Sarah's bed.

"Sorry, honey. I have to go by myself," replied Sarah.

"Why?"

"Because I miss my son Sam and my good friend June, and I want to spend time with them."

Ingrid shook her head showing no understanding of Sarah's remark. "But you told me your son died in a war."

"Yes, he did. He's buried in a pretty cemetery and I had a beautiful monument made to mark his grave. I used to visit the grave site almost every day," reminisced Sarah.

"But Sam can't talk to you. How can you visit?"

Sarah pulled Ingrid off her bed and threw her arms around the little girl. "I can't explain it, but he does talk to me. Maybe not with his voice, but I hear him."

"I'll miss you and so will Rusty," proclaimed Ingrid.

"Don't worry, Ingrid. I'll only be gone a few days."

_____

A bright sun rose on Friday making the day seem cheerful. *This is a good sign for my trip.*

Sarah had decided she didn't need a trunk for her clothes. A satchel would be enough. After all she would be coming back on Monday and she really wouldn't be going out in public while she was in Decatur. Visiting June and Sam's grave site did not call for an abundance of clothes.

After saying good-bye to Hilde, Ingrid, and, of course, Rusty, she walked to the nearby trolley. Carrying only a satchel made easy travel. She arrived at the station just in time to catch her train. She sat in a seat in the middle of the car, her favorite area.

So far everything is going just fine. I really think Madame Lily is wrong this time. I can't wait to see June, but first I'll have my taxi stop at Sam's grave.

Sarah enjoyed her train ride. Putting aside her bad memories of Decatur, she was happy to be going back to what had been home for almost twenty years. She went over in her mind the organizations she used to belong to. During World War I she had worked hard to raise money for the Red Cross .She became a nursing assistant in the flu pandemic of 1918. She helped build a home for widows and orphans. Her work all had one thing in common, helping people.

When the conductor came through her car yelling "Springfield next stop", she got nervous. This was it. It was really happening. She would be back in Decatur in about an hour.

As she got off the train, she was happy that she didn't have to wait for a trunk. She had her satchel and spotted a taxi not too far away. The taxi driver opened his door for her and asked if he could take her satchel.

"No, thank you. I'll keep it with me."

"Where to, lady?" asked the driver.

Sarah was getting so excited she could hardly speak, but she managed to say, "Please take me to Fairlawn Cemetery first." At last she would be able to see Sam's grave site and the beautiful monument that she had designed just for him. The monument she believed was a fitting tribute to his life.

The taxi went through the outside gate of the cemetery and the driver asked, "Where is the site you wish to visit?"

"Just keep on the main road and at the first intersection turn left," said Sarah as she noted things looked a bit different than when she was last here. But she knew the cemetery by heart. She could almost recite the names on most of the grave stones.

The taxi turned left at the first road and Sarah said, "Its right there." She pointed to a grassy space a few feet from the car. The driver stopped and Sarah looked around …confused. "Something is wrong. The grave should be right here. I know where I am and the monument should be here."

Sarah jumped out of the taxi and walked a few feet in one direction and few feet the other way. She then spotted the familiar name on a grave stone nearby. "Yes, this is where Sam is buried, but the monument is gone." Tears flooded her eyes but she was too upset to cry. "What could have happened to it?" She became hysterical.

The driver tried to help her get back into the car. Finally she got back into the back seat and told the driver to go to 3 Millikin Place. William must know what happened and she intended to find out. Not giving a thought of how William would receive her, she only wanted to know what happened to the monument.

On the ride to Millikin Place she still could not get her emotions under control. What if William had done something deliberately to destroy the Sam's grave? No, he would not have been that cruel. He thought a lot of Sam.

The taxi pulled into the driveway and Sarah was out of the cab before it totally stopped. She threw open the front door of the house which luckily was unlocked and ran into the front hall. Shouting, "William… William!"

CHAPTER 33

Ordained in the Stars

Decatur, Illinois 1933

A man came rushing into the hallway. "Excuse me, madam. May I help you with something?"

Sarah paid no attention to the man and continued to shout for William who finally appeared at the top of the stairs. He looked down at the hallway below and saw his servant, Garrison, trying to subdue a woman who was yelling and flapping her arms to get free of Garrison's grasp.

"What's going on down there?" William shouted and began to come down the stairs. As he got a little closer he recognized Sarah. "Sarah, calm down. Garrison, it's fine. Let her go."

Sarah did not clam down, but screamed at him, "What happened to Sam's monument?"

As irritated as he was with the intrusion, William realized Sarah had to be dealt with. Playing for time to think of what he could say to her, he suggested they go into the living room and sit down.

William's mind began reeling. When he had removed the monument 12 years ago, he had wanted some sort of revenge for the conduct of his former wife. Now looking into her eyes he could see that he was successful. She was obviously devastated and as yet didn't even know what his part had been in the monument's removal. Why didn't he feel triumphant?

Having no real option Sarah followed him into the living room. But when William motioned for her to sit on the couch, Sarah went over to the fireplace and, holding on to the mantle, turned to face him. "Did you take the monument away?" choked Sarah.

Garrison, who had still been standing in the hall, tried to make sure his employer was alright. The woman William called Sarah was totally unstrung. "Mr. Grady should I bring you some tea?"

Thankful for the interruption, he dismissed Garrison, "No. We are fine, Garrison."

William was silent for a minute trying to decide the best way to handle his ex-wife knowing that the grave site and monument were the dearest things in her life. She obviously had been to the cemetery and discovered the bare grave. He found himself unable to enjoy his revenge and he needed to calm Sarah down.

How thankful he was that Esther was in Chicago for the week-end and not there to witness this episode.

Sarah stood ridged against the fireplace waiting for William's explanation. She found herself hoping that William had some excuse for the bare grave. She would listen to what he had to say.

William walked over close to her. He would try to make her understand. "Well, Sarah, it was years ago when you left and may I remind you the circumstances under which you left were not ideal. I threw all your things out because I didn't want any memory of you around my house. Then I realized how much you loved Sam…"

At that point Sarah knew that William had indeed gotten rid of the monument. She snapped and went after him physically pushing him hard several times. In defense he pushed her back and she fell backward striking her head on the stone fireplace.

William kneeled down beside her body that lay lifeless on the hearth. "Sarah…Sarah. Oh, God! What have I done? Garrison, come in here. Bring me some ice and a towel. And I think there are some smelling salts in the bathroom. Hurry!"

Garrison who was still lingering in the hallway quickly went for the desired items. "Here, Mr. Grady, let me help." William, noting that her ever present hat was totally soaked in blood, gingerly took it off of her head and was amazed at all the blood on the hearth. He held the ice on her head and Garrison kept waving the smelling salts under her nose.

"Garrison, I don't think she's coming back. Look how she's bleeding. She's still out." William's voice was high and shrill showing his alarm.

Both men worked on her doing anything they could think of to bring her back to consciousness.

Finally Garrison said, "Mr. Grady, she's gone. I tried to get a pulse and got nothing. Should I call the hospital?"

"No, not yet." William stayed by her body and kept trying different techniques. He slapped her. Come on, darn you anyway!"

Finally Garrison was able to pull William away from the body. "She's dead."

"Are you sure? How do you know?"

"Mr. Grady, when I was a medic in the war, I had to deal with many dead bodies out in the field. Believe me. I know."

William sat down in a chair and looked at Sarah's body in disbelief, "I killed her."

Garrison said, "You didn't mean to. I saw the whole thing from the hall. She shoved you and you pushed her away. When you did she fell backwards and hit her head on the fireplace. That stone is so hard, Mr. Grady."

"Let's put her on the couch. Maybe she's not gone."

As they lifted the body, they saw a tremendous amount blood on the hearth.

"Mr. Grady, she is gone and if we put her on the couch it will also be a bloody mess."

"I can't think… I killed her… I didn't mean to…"

"I'm not sure how the police will look at this. I am a witness and can testify that it was an accident," volunteered Garrison.

William stared at Sarah's body while taking several deep breaths. He stumbled into a chair and set rigidly still.

Finally he spoke, "I'm not sure I want the police to know about this. They would ask questions I'm not prepared to answer. 'Who is she?' That would bring up our whole divorce scandal. 'Why was she so upset?' I don't want to tell them I destroyed the monument. Oh why did I destroy the monument? Because my wife was unfaithful to me and I wanted revenge. As President of Faries Manufacturing, I am known as a pillar of the community. I have a reputation to live up to. This would damage my image."

He stood over Sarah's body, just staring at it. He noted that the color was draining from her face. *You are still beautiful, Sarah. What went wrong with us? We were the perfect couple and worked so well together. After everything, I believe I still love you. I have missed you these last years. I didn't mean to hurt you.*

Garrison noticed the taxi waiting outside. "I'll go and dismiss the taxi and see what I can find out. Let me have some money to pay him."

As if in a dream, William reached in his pocket and pulled out a wad of bills for Garrison.

While paying the driver his fare, Garrison found that Sarah had arrived on the train from Chicago and had gone straight to the cemetery. The driver noted that she was extremely upset about the grave site and had asked to be driven to Millikin Place. "She forgot her satchel. I guess you can give it to her. I hope she is okay."

Back in the house William began to panic. "I don't want anyone to know she was here. Do you think the taxi driver will remember bringing her here? Oh, I can't think."

"Sit down and gather your thoughts, Mr. Grady. Between the two of us we can handle the situation."

Sitting down William said, "You're right. I'll sleep on it tonight and see what tomorrow brings."

Garrison looked kindly at his boss and said, "That won't work. We'll have to dispose of the body tonight. The hearth has to be scrubbed immediately so the stain can be lifted, and we have about two hours before rigor mortis sets in which makes the body hard to handle.

"Then, I hate to say this, but after a while the smell becomes atrocious. During my time as a medic in the army I saw horrible things.

I'm sorry to talk like this but we have to do something tonight. Sarah is gone; this is just a body."

Sensing he had to take charge Garrison asked, "What do you want to do with the body?"

William took a deep breath and said slowly, "Sarah always said that she wanted to be buried with Sam, so I guess the thing to do is to put her in Sam's grave."

"I think that's a good thing to do. We'll have to go to the cemetery tonight and dig her grave. If you'll go get an old blanket from upstairs, I'll get a couple of gunny sacks from the kitchen and we'll wrap her up."

William again stared for a minute at Sarah, noting the condition of her hat. She would be upset about her hat being destroyed. Then doing as he was told, he went upstairs to get the requested blanket and brought it down to the living room.

"You'll have to help me a little wrapping her body," said Garrison.

William kept telling himself," Garrison is right this is just a body. Sarah is gone."

The two men wrapped the body in the blanket and put a gunny sack on the top part and one on the bottom.

"Let me make sure the coast is clear and we'll take her to the car." Luckily Millikin Place is isolated from the rest of the city, so there was no one around. The men carried her to the car and placed her in the trunk.

By this time it was four o'clock in the afternoon. Garrison, fearing that William was about to break down, suggested that they have a snack and wait for it to get a bit darker outside. William appreciated the time to gather his thoughts, even though he could not eat anything.

In the meantime Garrison scrubbed the hearth. He went to the garage, put shovels in the car, and drove to the back door. They were ready to go.

CHAPTER 34

Sarah's Wish Fulfilled

Fairlawn Cemetery, Decatur 1933

Garrison and William got in the car about five in the evening and started driving to the cemetery. William was feeling a bit relieved. *This is going to work. Sarah will be with Sam and no one will know how it all happened.*

Suddenly Garrison stopped the car. "We have to go back. I forgot her satchel." He whirled the car around and they went back home.

William suddenly thought about her hat, "Don't forget her hat. I need to bury that with her. She always had a hat on."

William's mind was unsettled still and as they turned into the driveway he realized that Sarah would be with him forever. All he could see as they approached the house was Sarah and in his mind he could hear remarks she had made over the years. *This is my punishment. She will be with me constantly forever.*

Garrison grabbed her satchel and the hat from the house and they were off again.

As they pulled into the cemetery both men noted that no one was around and Decatur was sparsely settled around the area. No one would bother them.

It took almost four hours for them to dig down to Sam's coffin.

Garrison's shovel hit Sam's coffin and he exclaimed, "We've done it. Let's get the body and put it in the ground."

William who was not in as good a shape as Garrison, trailed behind but with the last ounce of his strength helped put Sarah and her hat and satchel into the ground.

Replacing the dirt did not take nearly as long as digging it out. In another two hours the ground above the graves was leveled. Garrison headed back to the car but William stood for a minute staring at the ground. Finally he whispered, "Sarah, you wished to be buried by your son. This is all I could do for you." The men got back in the car to head home.

William reflected, "Garrison, no one saw Sarah come to the house. She came straight to the house from the station and saw no one. No one saw us at the cemetery. I can only hope no one knew she was coming to Decatur, but even if they did, no one knew she was coming to see me. I think we have pulled it off. We are not involved in her disappearance. How can I ever thank you for helping me through this trauma?"

"No need to thank me. I saw what happened and it was an accident, but if we had gotten the police involved, they might have come to a different conclusion and there definitely would have been a scandal around the circumstance," said Garrison.

William had two days to get back to normal before his wife came home from Chicago. He was physically so worn out that he slept for several hours.

The next morning, he awoke to Garrison bringing him his breakfast and giving him the news that he would have to deal with a phone call from June Johns.

"June called this morning to ask if we had seen Sarah. She said that Sarah, who she had presumed dead, had called her and was expected to come yesterday and stay with her. She wondered if you had any news of her."

William panicked for a minute and then realized that June had no way of knowing that Sarah had come to his house. All he had to do was phone her and decline any knowledge of his former wife. He would show surprise that she even thought to call him.

Many of the people in Chicago would wonder what happened to her and some might call him, but again he could plead innocence of her whereabouts.

He got dressed and decided he had to go to the cemetery and say a proper good-bye to Sarah. Garrison who drove him to the grave site was not happy about it. "Someone could see you and question the newly dug dirt and wonder why you were there."

"I have to go. I need to apologize to both Sarah and Sam."

Arriving at the cemetery Garrison stayed in the car while William went to the site where they had buried her last night.

William got down on his knees and tried to pray. "God, you know I haven't prayed for a long time. But this is for Sarah. Please bless her and watch over her soul. All her life she tried to do things for other people. Don't judge her by the upset she had when we were having marital trouble. And…let her know that I am sorry for the trouble I caused both she and Sam. Sarah, I really loved you with all my heart."

William got back in the car. "Garrison, home please."

CHAPTER 35

Adjustment

Chicago, Illinois 1933

John Olsen stepped into his house almost smiling. After a very lucrative day at his office, he was ready for a pleasant dinner with his family.

"I'm home, honey," called John.

Hilde slowly came into the room. Her face radiated concern. "I'm worried, John."

"What's the matter? Is something wrong with Ingrid?"

"No. She's fine. But Sarah said she was coming back Monday...yesterday. She still isn't back and hasn't called to tell us she was delayed. That's not like her. I think something is wrong."

"Well, that doesn't sound like her but there's probably some simple explanation for it. Don't borrow trouble."

Hilde was quiet a moment, then said softly, "I just have a feeling."

Ignoring her, John called, "Let's go to dinner."

Bouncing into the dining room with Rusty by her side, Ingrid questioned, "Is Sarah back yet?"

"Not yet, but I'm sure she'll be here soon." replied Hilde.

"But where is she?" questioned Ingrid.

"We don't know right now, but I'm sure it's okay," said John.

Hilde had a little trouble getting Ingrid to bed. She read several books to her before Ingrid said, "I really miss Sarah," and fell asleep.

After two more days went by with still no word from Sarah, Hilde pressured John to call the hospitals, newspapers, and police in Decatur to see if they could get any information about Sarah. No one had been admitted to the hospitals fitting her description. The newspaper had no record of accidents since Friday. The police had not been in touch with anyone fitting Sarah's description.

After their investigation turned up nothing Hilde told John, "I can't believe we have no information about Sarah's life in Decatur. No friends, No organizations. We know nothing of her time there."

John said it was time to tell Ingrid that her Nanny, friend, and substitute grandmother may not be coming back.

"Why not? Why won't she come home? She said she would be back by my birthday and that's next week. Doesn't she love me anymore?" sobbed Ingrid.

Hilde tried her best to comfort Ingrid, but it wasn't possible.

"It's bedtime, honey. If Sarah were here she would tell you that she loves you and everything is going to be alright."

"I guess she would, but where is she?" asked Ingrid as she cried herself to sleep.

Hilde and John sat down with a glass of tea in their breakfast room where all important conversations took place.

"Since Sarah never told us about her life in Decatur, we know nothing except that she had a son named Sam who died in the war and a good friend named June. She obviously did not want us to know anymore. I believe if she could come home she would. She loved us," said Hilde.

"You're right. I'm sure she would contact us if she could. I wonder if she's dead," replied John.

"I haven't had a chance to tell you yet, but her friend Elizabeth called today and asked to talk to Sarah about her week-end in Decatur. I told her Sarah had not returned and that we have tried to find her without any success. Elizabeth said she feared the worst for her friend and believed something terrible had happened."

"Also, she said that Sarah went to an astrologist who told her it was ordained in the stars that she would not survive the trip," rambled Hilde choking up. "Should we go to the police and ask about her?"

"I don't think so. We know nothing about her life in Decatur. Sarah was a very private woman. If she had wanted us to know more about her life, she would have told us."

Deep in thought John ran his fingers around the edge of his glass. Finally he spoke, "Let's just remember her fondly. If she could have come back, I think she would have. Let's leave Sarah's return up in the air with Ingrid so she has more time to process her disappearance."

As the week-end approached Ingrid realized that Sarah might not be around. "Who is going to get Ruby? Sarah always brings her here for the week-end. When will Sarah be home?'"

Seeing how unhappy Ingrid was Hilde replied, "You and I can go get Ruby and bring her here for the week-end."

The week end unfolded as usual with Ingrid, Rusty, and Ruby playing together. Ruby's appearance took away part of the gloom that Ingrid was experiencing.

After the group was put to bed, John and Hilde sat in the breakfast room to continue their discussion. Hilde inhaled and began, "Sarah is never coming back, John. We may never know what happened to her. Ingrid, will recover because she has us, but I'm not sure Ruby ever will—well, ever will without us... Oh, John, Ruby loves Sarah and won't recover if she loses another loved one. Please, let's adopt her! Ingrid already thinks of her as a sister and I as a daughter." She reached for John's arm, awaiting his answer.

He smiled just a bit, placing his hand over hers. "I was thinking the same thing, Hilde. Adopting Ruby would help us all cope with Sarah's disappearance."

The next evening before Ruby was due to return to the orphanage, John and Hilde sat the girls down to give them the news. John spoke, "Girls, we want to officially make Ruby part of our family. Ruby, if it is alright with you, I'll go tomorrow to start the proceedings to adopt you."

The girls jumped up and down with joy. Through happy tears, Ruby exclaimed, "I'll have a new Mom and Daddy and sister!"

"Can she share my room? And..." Ingrid began, but suddenly stopped and became silent. After a quiet moment, she began again in a hushed tone, "Is Sarah ever coming home, Mama?"

Hilde looked at John searching for the words.

John cleared his throat and began. "Girls, I don't believe Sarah will ever come back here. I don't think she can... But I know she loved all of us. I believe Sarah is now at peace."

Ingrid spoke up right away, "Where is 'Peace'"?

Hilde took over, "Darling, 'Peace' is up in the sky by the stars where it is warm and sunny with family who are no longer on earth. Sarah can look down on you and watch as you grow into wonderful women."

Ruby nodded with understanding, "Sarah must be with her son Sam and my Mommy and Daddy! She said they all were up in the stars."

Hilde smiled and squeezed the girls close to her. "Yes, my loves. They are all finally together in the stars."

Fairlawn Cemetery

Decatur, Illinois 2016

"Hey, Al. You back here again?"

"Hi, Carl. I haven't seen you since I was here a year or so ago and now it seems like I am on the same errand."

"I remember. Some lady wanted you to witch a grave in this area."

"Right. And now she wants me to do it again."

"Doesn't she believe your first try?

"I don't know, but she said she really wants me to do it again. Something about her research."

The mature lady who had asked for the last report pulled up in her car. She got out and walked firmly to where Al stood by the large William Grady monument. Carl strolled several yards away from them, but still stood nearby out of curiosity.

"I know you are confused, Al, but I just want to confirm without a shadow of a doubt that this site holds who I think it does," said the lady. "Please tell me what you can about who is in the graves belonging to William Grady."

Al picked up his witching rod and repeated what he had done the last time. "According to the office there are three sites here that belong to Mr. Grady. Starting on the left…" Here Al paused as he walked across the grave. His rod fell to the right. "There is a man buried here." Continuing on Al walked across the second grave and declared, "There is a woman buried here."

The lady was visibly tense as Al walked across the last grave which was not marked. "There definitely is a woman buried here," he said as his rod fell to the left. "No doubt about it."

"Thank you so much. I had to be sure," said the lady as she reached in her purse to pay Al.

"I don't need any money, but I would like to know what you found out by knowing that there is a woman buried here in this unmarked grave."

The lady hesitated but then spoke to Al and Carl, who had come closer to them, "I thought I had found Sarah Grady when you did this last year. I was sure she was buried here, but after a little more research I found that she didn't die in 1921 like I thought. I found her living in Chicago until 1933, so I dug into her life deeper. I am now sure she is in this grave as I determined, but my timeline was off. She lived a whole new life after she left Decatur in 1921, until 1933 when her life was cut short and she was buried here. I just needed you to again assure me that a woman is buried here."

The lady put down a card on the grave site and walked away.

After she left, Al bent over to see what was written on the card:

```
REST IN PEACE
SARAH GRADY


YOU ARE NOT FORGOTTEN,
Mary Lynn
```

Made in the USA
Monee, IL
25 July 2023

39877281R00114